# Saving Baby

a novel by

Gregg Bell

# Epigraph

From caring comes courage. —Lao Tzu

# Chapter One

The baby was crying. Annie Rebarchek didn't even know if it was a boy or a girl. This whole interview process was psyching her out. It was like something out of a spy novel—she'd had to follow all these instructions, *do this and do that,* just to get to the interview. It had seemed simple enough at first. Her father had just insisted she get a summer job. Having a substantial summer job would make her applications to top colleges that much more attractive, especially in today's super-competitive environment. Annie had chafed at his demand—she wouldn't have minded a firm request—but what could she do, she was only seventeen, and like her father always said, 'If you live under my roof, you play by my rules.'

This baby kept crying. It was in a back room of the mansion somewhere. It might be on a different floor for all she knew. She wondered why nobody was comforting it, as it wasn't a colicky cry. It was a sad, a very sad cry, a lament. Not like Annie was an expert but she knew what hurt sounded like. She was intimidated to say anything to this man, her potential boss, Houston Monroe, but the baby's crying was making her so uncomfortable.

"So, Annie," Monroe said with a smirk as he leaned back in his ergonomic recliner. "What makes you think you can handle such a large responsibility?"

"Because I've been babysitting since I was thirteen, and well, because I've always been a very responsible person."

Monroe frowned. He was still handsome though, Annie thought, in his crisply white shirt and with his wavy, silver-ish hair. But oh, his baby crying.

"Annie, the position is not *babysitting*. It's being a domestic assistant."

"Sir—"

"Let me stop you right there. I'm going to insist that you call me Houston."

Annie bit the inside of her cheek. Calling Houston Monroe, Phoenix's billionaire environmentalist, by his first name was beyond her. But his baby crying was so sad. "Uh…"

"Houston." He looked her sternly in the eye.

She had no choice. "Houston."

"That's better."

"Houston, your baby is crying."

Monroe tilted his head at her, to the left, to the right. "Did you notice hearing aids in either of these ears?"

She exhaled and shook her head.

"Thank you," he said. "In other words, I can hear very well that Chase is crying, and let me assure you that Chase is fine, that he is in fact in *optimal* health. Now to return to my question. Are you prepared to handle the responsibilities of being a domestic assistant?"

Annie rolled back in her chair, forgetting it was on casters. Monroe's office was ultra modern: a jade-green Lucite oval desk, a long-armed chrome extender lamp over it. "Yes. Very much so. But the baby crying—"

"I told you Chase is *fine*."

"Sir—"

"Houston."

"Houston. Forgive me, but I'm telling you, your baby needs something. It's hurting."

Monroe stretched his long fingers behind his head and laughed as if he'd never heard anything more outlandish. He looked around at the Ming vases on his teak wood bookcases, at the photos of Phoenix's mayor and himself, of movie stars and himself, hanging on his office walls. His face grew severe. "Are you saying that you know what Chase needs better than I do?"

"No. Just that I know he needs something now."

He glowered. "Chase is learning discipline."

Annie gripped the arms of her chair, fingernails digging into the fine leather. Oh, he just wasn't getting it. Behind Monroe, Phoenix's city lights down in the valley were popping on like thousands of little starbursts. Annie was so frustrated with Monroe, but now she really wanted the job because if she got it she'd be able to comfort his baby. She gripped the chair even tighter.

"So you think you're mature enough to handle the position?" Monroe stated more than asked as he perused her job application and then flipped it onto the desk. "I must say your grades and references are superb."

Annie could barely hear him. All she could think about was comforting his poor baby who was wailing so sadly. "Can I see the baby?"

Monroe snorted out a laugh. "Want to see if he passes inspection?"

She shook her head quickly. "No. I just love babies."

* * *

The Monroe mansion. Annie couldn't help but gawk as Monroe led her through the living room: marble floors, Japanese-style low cocktail table, everything glass and chrome. They walked briskly past—Monroe giving no grand tour or descriptions—a computer room humming with monitors, and printers churning out documents. The room looked like it could've been the NASA command center. The house being so high-tech seemed out of place for the laid-back southwestern lifestyle most Arizonans embraced, but Monroe was known for being a perfectionist, obsessed with technology and insisting on the latest in everything. Annie remembered driving up the mountain, up the steep switchback road to get there. She'd had to put her KIA into the low gear just to make it. Monroe's mansion was a fortress-like building, brilliantly white, embedded in the red rock mountain, several rooms steeply cantilevered over the valley. Security cameras peeked out from seemingly everywhere and a twenty-foot-high cinder block wall surrounded the compound. Annie followed Monroe, his heels clicking on the buffed wood floors, through rooms tastefully decorated with abstract art.

Monroe turned into one of the cantilevered rooms. Floor-to-ceiling windows opened up a panorama of the Phoenix valley, an explosion of glitter now as the valley lights had come on full-force. Annie had lived her entire life in Phoenix, but still she'd never gotten used to cantilevered rooms and this one hung over a chasm that must've had a thousand-foot drop—and the baby's crib was right next to the window. A gray crib. No mobiles. No toys. No swaddling blankets. The baby was making little cough-like gasps, as if its throat and vocal cords were shot from incessant crying. He was thin, weakened, yellow-ish. Oh, Annie felt so sorry for him. Instinctively, she picked him up.

She plucked a facial tissue from the table next to the crib and wiped his tears. Instantly he stopped crying and clung to her. It was a good feeling—to hear his crying stop but also to feel another human being so warm and so close, another human being needing her so. "There now, that's better, isn't it?"

"You realize what you're doing is bad for him, don't you?" Monroe snatched the baby from her and planted him back in the crib.

Annie reached for the baby again but Monroe held her back. “Hey!” she called, resenting his touching her.

Monroe released her but said, “Chase needs to learn discipline. He’s not going to end up a wishy-washy lump of out of control desire like the rest of humanity.” He smiled but it was an empty smile. “There’s too many of those around as it is.”

“But he’s a baby.”

“The most formative period.”

Chase started crying again.

“He just needs to be held, Mr. Monroe. To be reassured. He needs human contact. He needs love.”

Monroe laughed. “Well, I can see you’re not going to work out.” He started out of the room, apparently assuming Annie would follow.

She didn’t. Despite not looking well, Chase had handsome little features, beckoning blue eyes, but he had significantly darker skin than Monroe’s.

Monroe stopped in the middle of the room next to a white satin sofa. “Miss Rebarchek!”

Annie gasped for a breath. Monroe had a reputation for being brash, but even so, rejecting her so suddenly caught her off guard. Fine, she decided. She could live without the job, but this baby… this baby that just needed love…love she was so ready to give it. She was on the verge of crying herself. “Mr. Monroe, I can really do this job.”

“Oh, you think so? Well, you’ve just proved to me you can’t.” He nodded for her to follow. “Now please leave.”

Her reflex was to obey. All her life she’d lived in submission to male authority figures. In fact, Monroe reminded her of her father. She stepped toward him but then stopped. She wasn't leaving this baby in this situation. "Mr. Monroe, please, give me a chance."

"I have and you blew it."

"I can do this job. And I can do it the way you want it done." Maybe she was lying but she didn't care. She just wanted to help the baby.

Monroe touched his chin. He ran his hand through his hair.

It was an opening and Annie knew it. "I'll do whatever you want me to."

His eyes crawled all over her.

She didn't like the way he looked at her. It was a sly, indirect look, not like the lustful leers from the horny jocks at Alameda High where she went to school, which were bad enough in their own right but at least they were direct. Okay, she decided she could handle Monroe's look. She could handle it to help the baby.

* * *

After the interview Annie drove to the Target by Desertback Community College. The department store was the unofficial hangout of the kids at Alameda High. She met her friend Tara, who was sitting with Stu, a new kid who'd just moved there from Texas, in the little Starbucks within the store. Stu was a big, strong kid—Tara said he was a wrestler—slow to speak and when he spoke he had a deep, rich voice with a Texas drawl. Word was he knew a lot about computers and was nice. Annie was glad to see someone as mega-popular as Tara hanging with a relative outsider. She walked up to them.

Tara popped up from her chair and hugged her. "Oh my God, Annie!"

The hug reminded Annie of little baby Chase clinging so

tightly to her. "Hey, Tara."

"Annie." Tara nodded toward Stu. "Do you know Stu?"

Annie waved. "Hey, Stu."

Stu offered a shy smile.

"We'll be right back, Stu." Tara gave Stu a quick nod, took Annie's elbow and walked off with her. "So tell me all about it! You were actually in his house? Houston Monroe! Oh my God!"

"It wasn't a house, Tara. It was a mansion. The place was huge. And way up on Sagebrush Mountain, all these rooms cantilevered over the valley. I was getting dizzy."

"So what's he like? Is he as handsome as he is on TV?"

Annie shrugged, remembering the lusty look he'd given her at the end. "He was all right, I suppose."

"Oh my God!" Tara grabbed her elbow. "Houston Monroe! Yeah, he's old, but he's good-looking and a *billionaire!*"

"He's not that old. I'd say mid-thirties."

"Did he talk about global warming and *wiping out the brown cloud*, all that, like he does on TV?"

Annie shook her head.

"So did you get the job? Come on. Spill."

Annie shrugged. "I don't know. He said he'd call."

"Oh my God! Houston Monroe! You might be working for Houston Monroe!"

* * *

When Annie got home she knew her father would be waiting for her. He was always waiting for her. She tossed her backpack onto the stairs and heard him call her name. She headed for the den.

"And so." He looked up from his *Wall Street Journal*. "How did it go?"

The TV was on, a business show, the stock market ticker

running on the bottom of the screen. The den was comfortable. It was her father. A green-cloth recliner sat in front of the TV, her father planted in it. Bookshelves, filled with just about every business success book ever written, lined the walls. Annie settled on an ottoman at his feet. “It went okay.”

“Well, that explains it,” he said with a friendly smirk.

Annie shrugged. She knew him so well. Knew he was so impressed by business success. But she knew he loved her too and since her mother died she’d come to rely more and more on his love. “For the most part it was good, Daddy. He was nice and his home was incredible.” Still she felt terribly uncomfortable about the situation the baby was in.

“Not surprising, Annie, Houston Monroe is one of the richest men on earth. He owns Green Magic Waste Removal, half the wind farms in the country and sits on the boards of Fortune 500 companies.”

“Yeah, Dad, I know. You’ve only told me about a thousand times.”

“You can learn a lot from a man like that, honey. And to have that connection…it could turn out to be priceless.”

And Monroe might turn out to be a perv, she was thinking. But the thing she couldn’t get out of her head was poor little Chase. A billionaire’s kid and he looked like he was dying—and the way he was crying so sadly. Oh! “Yeah, I’m sure I’d learn something.”

“Honey, Monroe’s a business genius. He started out with one garbage truck—that he drove!—and he parleyed it into an international empire.”

Annie thought of that Nine Inch Nails song with the line *you could have it all: my empire of dirt*. But the baby. It was all about the baby. She didn't know what was going on with his being so neglected but it couldn't be good—and might be evil. It was as if during that brief hug she'd shared with him, his little body was transmitting the message *Help me!* "You know that success stuff doesn't really matter to me."

Her father raised his eyebrows and frowned. "Well, what did he say? Did you get the job?"

She so wanted to tell him about the baby's crying, its poor health, its being neglected. "He didn't say much of anything really. He said he'd call."

"But what sense did you get from him?"

"Truthfully?" She caught his eye. "That he wasn't a very good father."

"Really?"

"I don't know." She looked at her fingernails, Aruba Aqua with sparkles this week. "His baby was just crying and crying and when I picked him up, he grabbed him from me and put him back down."

"Annie, babies cry." He smiled. "You were a bit of a champion crier yourself."

"Yeah yeah. So you've told me."

He set the paper down and muted the TV. "Well, I would have to think that Monroe knows what he's doing."

"That makes one of us. And anyway, I don't have to get that job. I can always work with Tara at the summer day camp again."

"Annie, what you do this summer will be critically important for your acceptance to top colleges. You can work at the day camp next summer if you want. Then it won't matter. You'll already be in. But if you have that you worked for Monroe on your transcript that can only bode really well. How many applicants can say they worked for *Houston Monroe?*"

"But what if he's a creep?"

"What do you mean?"

She remembered the lustful leer he'd given her. "Oh, I don't know. I just didn't get the greatest vibe from him."

"Like he might be..." He hesitated. "...you know, coming on to you?"

She shrugged.

"Well, if that's the way you feel, you don't go back. No matter what."

"Oh, it's really more about the baby, Dad. It just seemed so sad."

"Honey, like I said, babies cry."

# Chapter Two

That night Annie dreamed of a baby tumbling down a mountainside. Tumbling, glancing off cacti and boulders, crying, gathering speed. She jerked awake. It wasn't even five in the morning. She felt like the dream was telling her that she was needed at Monroe's and that she'd get the job.

Later that morning she got a text from Monroe: *Thanks but won't be needing you*. Well, so much for her dream, but what a lousy way of letting her know. Her father was going to be so disappointed. She was disappointed too. Not because she wouldn't be working for Monroe but because she wouldn't be able to help baby Chase.

Oh well. In the kitchen, she popped a toaster pastry into the microwave. She supposed getting the job just wasn't meant to be. She bit into the toaster pastry. She couldn't even taste it. Baby Chase really needed help. That hug he'd given her *had been* a cry for help.

She couldn't even finish her breakfast. She ran out to her KIA and drove back to Monroe's mansion. She got as far as the perimeter gate, a bank of swiveling surveillance cameras eying her suspiciously. She leaned out and hit the intercom button on a post.

"Yes?"

"Mr. Monroe, it's Annie Rebarchek."

"I can see that."

"Well, I got your text—"

"Which was self-explanatory."

Annie swallowed hard and could feel herself getting ready to put the KIA into reverse. It was the submission to male authority figure thing again. But she couldn't stop thinking about baby Chase. He was being abused. He was suffering. Maybe dying. "Well, sir, I don't think you gave me a fair chance yesterday."

"Oh really?"

She took a deep breath. "Really." She took another. "I can do the job, sir. And I can do it the way you want it done."

Silence. And more silence. Annie told herself to wait. To just keep waiting. She gritted her teeth. After a minute that seemed like an hour, the huge electrified gate swung open. She drove up the drive.

She parked near the back entrance, checked herself in the rear view mirror and climbed out. It would be what it would be, she told herself, but at least she was doing her best to try and help Chase. Her conscience demanded no less. Up the stairs she went to the fancy entrance, two marble pillars—Monroe seemed to have a thing for marble—flanking Christmas-red double doors with brass handles. She squared her shoulders and rang the doorbell.

Her heart throbbed as she waited. What was she getting herself into? One of the doors swung open. A young man, late twenties maybe, in a gray linen suit and light gray shirt nodded her in. The man was white but decidedly dark-ish, had long brown hair in a ponytail and a hip, scruffy chin beard. "Follow me."

Annie was dying to ask who he was. He was definitely rich or at least he dressed rich. What was he doing there? She shook her head and told herself to stay focused. This was all about Chase. The man led her through several rooms—Annie was glad not to hear crying—up to Monroe's office. Monroe was typing something into his phone.

She waited.

He set the phone on his desk. “What can I do for you, Ms. Rebarchek?”

Great, she thought. She’d gone from being *Annie* to *Miss Rebarchek* to *Ms. Rebarchek*. Next she’d probably be *hey you*. But she just kept telling herself to be strong for Chase. “Mr. Monroe, I want the domestic assistant job.”

Monroe laughed.

“Sir, just give me a chance. That’s all I ask. Let me prove to you that I can do the job.”

He leaned back in his recliner and seemed to be sizing her up. He took his time. “As you might imagine, one of the traits I look for in people is courage.”

Annie swallowed. She didn’t consider herself courageous, far from it. It was just her concern for Chase emboldening her. “Okay.”

“And you’re showing me something here today. How old are you, Annie?”

She shrugged. He knew how old she was from her application, and now he was calling her *Annie* again. Confusing. “Seventeen.”

He nodded. “Not bad. Not bad at all.”

She was on the verge of asking about Chase. It was crazy but the longer she was there, the more she was thinking that there might be a bad reason for him not crying. “I’ll take good care of your son, Mr. Monroe. I’ll treat him like he was a member of my own family.”

“I believe you would.” He rose from the recliner. “Yes, you’ve shown me something here today. Unfortunately, I’ve already hired someone else."

Oh. Annie thought of the young guy in the gray suit. Could Monroe have hired him? It seemed unlikely. But here she was again—out and unable to help Chase. Chase who *needed* help. "I…I don't know what to say."

"There's nothing to say." He looked toward the door. "Dr. Hakim!"

"What about Chase?" Her voice trembled.

"What about him?"

The handsome young man in the gray suit stepped into the room.

"Is he okay?"

Monroe laughed—and so did the young man. "Good luck to you, Annie. I'm sure you'll find a good position somewhere. If I hear of anything, would you like me to give them your number?"

"But Chase…"

* * *

Annie cried all the way on the ride home. She felt so sorry for poor little Chase. Her gut churned. Why had Monroe let her into the compound if he'd already hired someone else? It was like he'd set her up to knock her down. All she wanted was to help Chase. She was feeling a connection with him, a desire to protect him, and the feeling was growing stronger.

She went to a park near her house and sat on a bench by a pond. Inline skaters cruised by on an asphalt path. Kids were fishing, casting their lines in broad arcs over the shiny water. The sun was still rising and Annie could feel its power on her skin, the day's heat moving in. Soon the temperature would climb into the hundreds, and the people would disappear indoors into air conditioning. She gazed vacantly into the distance. Chase. She didn't know if she could handle her feelings of not being able to help him. She was young, yes. She had friends, yes. High hopes for a good life. But suddenly she was consumed with concern for a little baby that she'd held for just barely a minute.

She went home, the house empty. Her father must be out on a sales call. She had the house, possibly for the whole day, to herself but the freedom afforded her no pleasure. Her life suddenly seemed long and hard.

* * *

That night, Annie tossed and turned. She told herself she'd done what she could, that she needed to let her concern for baby Chase go—but to no avail. She reminded herself of what her father had said. *Babies cry*. She supposed it was possible she was letting her imagination run away with her, exaggerating everything. Monroe was Chase's father after all. Certainly he had Chase's best interest at heart. That Monroe was quirky and had an unusual way of doing things, okay. Quirky and unusual did not equate with abusive. Monroe was the pride of the valley and darling of the media. A rags-to-riches story. An eco-crusader out to rid the valley of pollution and the infamous 'brown cloud' of smog hanging over it.

Annie continued to toss. Her mind had all the arguments as to why she should stop worrying, but the one thing she couldn't overcome was that cry for help she'd felt when she'd held Chase. Maybe it was crazy but she'd felt it. She couldn't deny it.

Would the rest of her life be like this? she wondered. Not able to have any peace? She was too young to be troubled like this. She'd just needed a summer job. Now little Chase's woeful crying had taken up residence in her heart.

Somehow, some way, just before dawn she fell asleep. She

wasn't surprised when she woke to find she'd slept through getting a text. She checked her phone. It was from Houston Monroe: *You start Monday morning.*

* * *

Annie needed to keep this low-key. If word got out she was working for Monroe, it could go viral with her social platform friends. Then who knew what sort of favors or inside information they would be looking to get from her. She had to tell Tara, hands-down her best friend, of course and her father.

She waited for her father to come back from playing golf. She knew that was the best time to talk to him because he was always happy then. He was in the garage taking his clubs out of his Volvo's trunk. The Arizona dry heat poured into the garage even though it was only ten in the morning.

"So," Annie said, stepping down the two stairs from the house into the garage. "Did you win?"

He shut the trunk and laughed. "As a matter of fact I did. Micky Lahart is the club champion but I managed to take him down two and one."

Annie smiled. She never knew the specifics of golf terminology. It was so confusing. All she knew about golf was Tiger Woods. "Well, congratulations."

"Thanks, honey. Now I just hope he doesn't stop using me because of that."

"Would he do that?" Annie knew that with her father ultimately business success was more important than golf, more important than just about anything really.

"No, I don't think so. I've had his account for years."

"Dad."

He turned to her. His blue shirt was sweaty around the collar.

He pushed the visor on his head back. "Yes, honey."

"I got the nanny job at Monroe's."

"Oh." His face fell. "I thought you were having second thoughts about that." He turned away and wiped his clubs with a towel.

His reaction surprised her. She thought he'd be thrilled. "You know, I figure it's just for the summer." He still wasn't looking at her. Not like him at all. "And like you said, the connection with him might be priceless."

"Annie, I've been thinking about you working for Monroe, and since I didn't hear anything from you, I assumed you didn't get the job. Anyway." He set the towel on his clubs and turned back to her. "I don't want you working for him."

"What!" She thought of Chase. Of how he needed her.

He clenched his jaw. "You can't take the job."

"But why? You were so excited about it."

"I was, that's right." He nodded. "Until you told me Monroe was coming on to you, and, honey, I'm not going to let you into that situation."

"But I told you it was more about the baby."

"That doesn't matter. You're not working there."

"But I already accepted. I *have to* do it now." She had to help Chase is what she had to do.

"You don't *have to* do anything, Annie. Anyway that's my final answer—you're not working for him."

"Oh my God, Dad, you're treating me like I'm a child. I know what I'm doing."

"I know what I'm doing too, and the fact of the matter is that as long as you're living under my roof, you're playing by my rules. End of discussion."

# Chapter Three

Mrs. Kendall was not the most popular teacher at Alameda High. She wasn't down with the kids about the latest memes, wouldn't discuss the super-hot TV shows and act hip like some of the other teachers. What set Mrs. Kendall apart in Annie's eyes though was that Mrs. Kendall cared about her. Ever since Annie's mom died it was like Mrs. Kendall was mom number two. Mrs. Kendall had given Annie her phone number and Annie called and went to see her.

Mrs. Kendall taught English Lit and she was the most knowledgeable person Annie knew. Annie rang the bell outside her apartment. Such a pretty woman, Annie thought when Mrs. Kendall opened the door. Soft curls in her hair, tinged prematurely gray at the hair line. Gorgeous white teeth. Liquid brown eyes. A gentle smile.

"Annie, how nice to see you again. Come right on in. Please, have a seat."

Annie smiled and walked past her. Part of her felt guilty. She only came to see Mrs. Kendall when she had problems to ask about, which didn't seem fair. She did feel safe with her though and oh, her apartment was so lovely, like a Van Gogh painting. Beautiful beige floral wallpaper with impressionist prints hanging on the walls. A mint green sofa with purple throw pillows. A glass cocktail table loaded with books and flanked by two brass candle holders with lit candles, the candles filling the room with luscious vanilla scent and soft ambient light. Just to be in the apartment was to relax. But Annie knew this visit wasn't about relaxation. "Thanks." She sat on the sofa.

Mrs. Kendall eased into a tan armchair. “So how is the summer going for you?”

Annie ran through a quick sketch of her life. Everything she *hadn't* come to talk about. Finally they both seemed to know it was time for her to share what was tearing her up inside. Mrs. Kendall seemed to ask her with her eyes.

“Mrs. Kendall, I feel like I’m stuck between a rock and a hard place.” Annie told her of getting the job with Houston Monroe, her father forbidding her taking it and, lastly, about her overwhelming concern for baby Chase.

Mrs. Kendall said nothing. She just looked on with accepting eyes.

Then Annie dropped the bomb. “Mrs. Kendall, you know I’ve struggled my whole life with the male authority issue, and it scares me more than I can say, but I’m going to disobey my father’s command and take that job at Houston Monroe’s.”

Mrs. Kendall inhaled deeply and put her hand to her mouth.

* * *

Annie wasn’t thrilled with Mrs. Kendall’s reaction but she wasn’t surprised by it either. Annie had gone to her for the truth, and the truth, Mrs. Kendall said, was that there was no easy answer to the situation. She asked Annie what *she* felt the right thing to do was. She said that the answer could only be found within. Hmm. Looking at it that way, Annie thought, the answer was easy—she had to help baby Chase.

She drove to the Target to meet Tara. Annie knew she could trust Tara, but now she was going to be asking for more than Tara’s trust.

Annie was glad Tara was alone. It was so easy to meet up with friends at the Starbucks inside the Target. Tara was sipping an iced coffee, looking at her phone, and when she saw Annie she jumped up and gave her a hug.

"Come on, Tara," Annie said. "Let's walk."

"Should I bring my coffee?"

Annie nodded.

They walked alongside the pharmacy, aisles loaded with vitamins, bandages and drugs. Annie said, "I see you've been hanging with Stu a lot lately. Anything going on between you two?"

"Nah." Tara shook her head. "He's just the sweetest guy though." She laughed. "He's this country boy, and he's got all these 'yes'm' and 'I reckon' things he says, and he talks *so slow*. I think he's putting me on half the time but he's not."

"Well, that's cool. Sounds like he's just being himself."

"It's funny you asked about him." Tara hesitated.

"What do you mean?"

"Because he asked about you. Not in a hitting on you way. At least I don't think."

Annie smiled. Stu did seem nice. "Anyway, Tara, back to why I wanted to talk to you."

"Okay."

Annie nodded. "I got the nanny job."

"Oh my God!" Tara hugged her. "You're working for Houston Monroe!"

Annie looked around. "Not so loud."

"Yeah yeah. Gotcha. But Houston Monroe!" she whispered, her face going red. "You're working for Houston Monroe!"

"There's more."

"He's giving you a Mercedes to drive the tyke around in?"

Annie laughed. "No, not yet anyway, but I need your help

with something."

"Sure. Name it."

"Cover for me?"

"You mean not tell anybody you're working for Monroe?"

"No." Annie caught her friend's eye. "I need you to cover for me with my father. He forbid me to take the job, and I'm going to tell him I'm working with you at the summer camp."

"Oh." Tara rubbed the back of her neck.

"I know it's a lot to ask."

Tara ran her hand across a mannequin's orange linen skirt as they passed through the women's section. "So you want me to lie is what you're saying?"

Annie frowned. "Hopefully it won't come to that." She bit the inside of her cheek. "But if it does, yes."

* * *

It had been hard asking Tara to cover for her. It had been even harder lying to her father. (At least she'd made it convincing, telling him she was going to have to buy all kinds of things for camp on the credit card he'd given her. He said okay. He just wanted to see the receipts.) The hardest thing of all though had been worrying about little Chase. Now, finally, Monday morning rolled around. Annie brushed her teeth. She could smell the coffee brewing in the kitchen. Her dad would be downstairs having his usual Danish before heading off to his consulting job. She was debating waiting till he left but if she waited, she risked being late at Monroe's. She grabbed her summer camp backpack and stomped down the stairs.

"Morning, honey." Her father looked nice in a navy blue suit. As usual he was poring over the *Wall Street Journal*. "You have everything you need? Did you go over last year's checklist?"

Annie rolled her eyes. "Yes, Dad. Got everything. I've been doing this for two years now already."

"I know. I know. Just double checking." He looked at his watch. "Hey, is Mr. Carr still running the camp?"

Annie shrugged. "As far as I know. It didn't say in the email."

He checked his watch again. "What time you supposed to be there?"

"Eight-fifteen."

"Perfect." He finished a last bite of the Danish. "I'm going to drop you there. I want to say hi to Mr. Carr, and then Tara can drive you home."

"Uh."

"Come on. Hurry or you'll be late. Me too." He dabbed a napkin to his lips.

"Uh."

"What?"

"The car Tara was going to use is in the shop. I have to pick her up."

He searched her eyes.

"It is."

He sighed. "All right. Did you remember to get the oil changed in the KIA?"

"Yes, Dad."

"Just remember: no goofing around in the car. Our insurance is high enough as it is."

"Yes, Dad."

"Now I've got to get going." He kissed her on the forehead and headed out the door.

What's next, Annie thought. She really didn't need all this

drama. She was worried enough about Chase—and facing Monroe, and maybe this Dr. Hakim, whoever the heck he was. She waited until she was sure her father was gone and headed over to Monroe's compound.

Up the winding switchback road she drove, the KIA's engine straining, Monroe's compound looming larger and larger with each pass. The compound was so white it stood out brilliantly against the red rock mountain. Of course being white it didn't draw the sun's rays, and Monroe being so into environmentalism, that was certainly by design, but the compound also had the vibe of being a fortress, an outpost maybe, a prison even. As if the air was getting thinner the higher she rose, Annie found herself taking deeper and deeper breaths. She turned off the radio. She checked that her phone was on vibrate. Her hands were shaking. Maybe her father was right—she shouldn't be there. But it was Chase's hug, Chase's little body crying out to hers *help me* that was giving her courage.

The perimeter gate swung open without her even activating the intercom. That was something that had been established early—at Monroe's she felt like somebody was always watching her. She drove up the steep driveway to the gaudy double-door entrance flanked by the marble pillars. It was an entrance that said, 'You are about to enter the halls of the mighty.' She killed the engine. And she was the non-mighty. Not that she wanted things to be that way but for now that's the way they were. It had just always been a major challenge for her to stand up to men, especially men in positions of authority. Her mother had been the same way. Everything had always come down to what Annie's father had said. When Annie was brutally honest with herself she felt that her mother's subservience had hastened her death. For her mother had been an ambitious woman with an intense life urge, but her father's dominance had always kept her down.

Annie climbed out of the KIA and made her way to the double doors. When her mother died, Annie had sworn she'd never succumb to male authority. It was her solemn promise. So far she hadn't been able to keep it. She rang the doorbell.

Monroe opened the door. He wore white slacks and a white open-collar shirt. He smiled warmly. Maybe this wouldn't be so bad, Annie thought.

"Welcome," he said, waving her in.

"Thank you." Annie caught a whiff of his exquisite cologne as she walked by. "I must admit I was surprised to hear from you, but also very pleased." She heard the door close firmly behind her. She turned and Monroe was entering a security code into an alarm system. He looked at her.

"Well, I'm happy to welcome you aboard. I pride myself on putting together an awesome team."

Team? Annie thought. This was new. "Okay."

"And without further ado let me take you in to meet Dr. Hakim."

Annie thought for a minute. Dr. Hakim. The handsome young ponytailed guy from before. Things were suddenly looking a little less favorable.

Monroe led her to a sitting room off the living room, still on the first floor. The mansion seemed endless. The sitting room was bright with the morning sun. Its wall facing the valley was a floor-to-ceiling window. A pit group sofa sat around a square cocktail table, a laptop open on it, Dr. Hakim sitting behind it. On the back wall was a black and white version of Michelangelo's 'spark' painting of God reaching down to touch Adam.

"Dr. Hakim," Monroe began, "I'm sure you remember Annie from the other day, but now by way of formal introduction, please meet Annie Rebarchek."

Dr. Hakim rose, stepped toward Annie and offered his hand. "It's a pleasure," he said with an accent and a smile.

Annie shook his hand. The guy was obviously friendly enough but she wanted to know what was going on with the 'team' concept and how it was going to affect Chase. "Nice to meet you, doctor."

"Please." Monroe gestured. "Let's all sit."

They settled into the pit group, Annie making sure to sit plenty far, but not obnoxiously so, from them. As she gathered herself she again realized that she didn't hear Chase crying, which was comforting and yet at the same time disconcerting.

Dr. Hakim turned the laptop toward Monroe. "Another academic study on child-rearing practices in Sub-Saharan Africa. It's about children being a gift from God and how tribal elders transmit their wisdom to them."

Monroe held the top of the laptop as he read. Then he said, "Sounds like Hillary Clinton's 'It takes a village.'"

"Exactly," Dr. Hakim said.

Again, Annie thought, maybe things wouldn't be so bad.

Then Dr. Hakim said, "And it's been an utter disaster."

The harshness with which Dr. Hakim spoke this last made Annie shudder. Her palms were sweating. Again she thought maybe her father was right—she shouldn't be there. Maybe she should just bail. But concern for Chase was keeping her from doing so. She couldn't leave him there under those dire circumstances.

"Annie," Monroe said familiarly, "Dr. Hakim is an expert in

child rearing from Cairo University in Egypt. He is going to be overseeing Chase's developmental program."

Annie found herself reflexively nodding and yet feeling very uncomfortable with what she was hearing. Dr. Hakim was from Egypt. Maybe she was over-reacting but if this was about that drastic Sharia law the terrorists were trying to force on everyone… She turned to Doctor Hakim. "So what exactly is the plan for Chase's development?"

"That's what we're working out now, Annie," Dr. Hakim said, saying her name tentatively, as if he was aware he was taking a risk of being overly-familiar by calling her by her first name so soon. "Do you have some input for us already?"

Annie breathed in deep and sat up. "I think Chase needs love."

"Ah, ah," said Dr. Hakim. "I couldn't agree more." He looked at Monroe and then at Annie. "It's just a question as to *how* the child is given love."

"Babies need to be held." Annie could feel her face flushing. "They need to be touched."

Dr. Hakim's tone turned sharp again. "And what, perhaps, are you basing this claim of yours on? What data do you have to back it up?"

"I don't need data." She felt like she was beet red.

Monroe said, "Annie, Dr. Hakim has three doctorates in child developmental research."

Annie looked Dr. Hakim in the eye. "So what do you think Chase needs?"

Dr. Hakim rubbed his little chin beard, then glanced at the laptop. "Chase needs discipline."

Annie wanted to tell them both that they were clueless, that

Chase just needed love. But she remembered how Monroe had shut her down before, and for Chase's sake she didn't want that to happen again. She took another deep breath and forced herself to remain silent. She had deceived her father to do good. She would deceive Monroe and Dr. Hakim to do the same.

"Studies have shown," Dr. Hakim said, "that the most well-adjusted children are those who were raised *from infancy* under a strict moral code. A code like Maat."

Annie frowned.

"Annie," Monroe said, "trust me—Dr. Hakim knows what he's talking about."

This couldn't be good, Annie thought. "So what is Maat?"

"Maat is order, divine order," Dr. Hakim said. "Without Maat is Isfet: chaos, violence."

Oh God. This was really sounding like that Sharia law. And she wanted to see Chase. She was uncomfortable with him not being mentioned. "Where's Chase?"

"He's not here," said Monroe. "I felt we could be more objective if we were alone."

Annie was suspicious. "Well, where is he?"

Monroe rose from the sofa. "With his mother."

# Chapter Four

Annie's head was so full of all the things that took place at Monroe's she barely remembered to preserve her cover story with her father that she was working at the summer day camp with Tara. So before she got home, she parked the KIA and jogged around the park near her house, got some grass stains on her knees, disheveled her hair, anything to make it look like she'd been working at the camp. All she could think about though was this Dr. Hakim and his Maat and Isfet. Scary stuff. Like that Sharia law. Yet, Monroe had seemed sincere in wanting to do his best by Chase. How could he be so blind? And Chase was with his mother! Annie laughed as she got in her car and left the park. How amazing that she could have forgotten that Chase had a mother. It was as if Monroe's billions and celebrity had obliterated the notion that an ordinary human woman could've given birth to the offspring of such a larger-than-life personage like Monroe. Perhaps it was because Annie didn't have a mother any more herself. At times it seemed the world consisted of only men.

Anyway, no complaints or suspicion from her father when she got home. Just the usual 'how did it goes' while glued to his *Wall Street Journal*. She made up a story or two to make her answers believable. She wasn't happy that she had to keep deceiving him, but she was doing what she had to do.

She went online and learned all she could about Maat. Thank God it wasn't Sharia law but it wasn't anything good either. It was ancient, occult. Sun gods and pharaohs. She didn't know what to make of it.

She met Tara at a convenience store. They got iced teas and went walking on a multi-purpose path that ran along a golf course. Annie loved Tara. Definitely her best friend for life. She just wasn't sure she could trust her with something as sensitive and bizarre as all that was happening at Monroe's. Annie could see down the road though and knew she'd eventually have to talk to somebody about it.

Tara did her usual flipping out over Annie being at Monroe's. Annie let her go on until she settled down. "Tara, can I tell you something in complete confidence?"

"Of course." She sipped her drink.

The path lights were coming on as the last golfers straggled off the course. The lights were time sensitive and flashing intermittently like fireflies. The mountains surrounding the valley looked like storm clouds on the horizon. Finally the heat was dying down. "I mean," Annie said, "you have to swear you won't tell a soul."

"Well, now that you put it that way, maybe you shouldn't tell me. You're starting to sound like you're going to tell me you murdered somebody or something."

Annie laughed. Not yet I haven't, she thought. "It's nothing like that but it is very important."

"Tell me then."

Annie told her everything.

The pair walked along in silence for a few minutes, a breeze, still warm, wafting in their faces. Finally Tara spoke.

"I gotta tell you, Annie, what you just told me creeps me out. Especially the occult stuff. I'm taking Mr. Wen's sociology class on ancient religions and some of it's about the ritual sacrifice of babies."

"Tara, please."

"I'm serious. A lot of those ancient religions did it, and you can even look at stuff today with Christian Scientists denying their babies medical care *and the babies die*."

This wasn't what Annie was wanting to hear. But maybe it wasn't as off the wall as it seemed either. Perhaps Monroe wasn't denying Chase medical care, but he was denying him love and without love Chase was dying.

* * *

There was only one thing to do. Annie raced home and studied online all she could about what it took to raise a healthy baby, feverishly jotting down sources in a notebook. Dr. Hakim had asked what she was basing her claims on—she would tell him. When she was done online, she went to a twenty-four-hour Walmart and bought a sound machine, mobiles for the baby's crib and swaddling blankets. She formulated a rudimentary plan, then, mind racing, emotions churning, utterly exhausted, she dropped off to sleep.

In the morning she drove to Monroe's compound.

Feeling like the information she was armed with was so sensible, and so documented by reliable sources, she was confident Monroe and Dr. Hakim would be open to changing their course with Chase. She grabbed her notebook but decided to leave all the things she'd bought for Chase in the car. She didn't want to seem pushy.

Dr. Hakim met her at the door. The man truly was handsome and always so elegantly dressed. Today a beige cotton suit. He wore clothes so fluidly. Her mind shifted quickly though to the task at hand as she heard Chase crying.

"Is Chase okay?" she said, hurrying ahead of Dr. Hakim,

following the sound of Chase's crying to his room. Dr. Hakim was saying something about meeting in the living room but all Annie could really hear was Chase's crying.

She shook her head as she walked into the cantilevered room, feeling a rush of vertigo as she caught sight of the valley so far down below. Chase, once again, was all alone. She went to him but before she could pick him up, Dr. Hakim grabbed her arm.

Monroe walked in. "What's going on here?"

"I just wanted to see Chase," Annie said, breathing hard. "To see if he's okay."

Dr. Hakim released her.

"Follow me," Monroe ordered and he marched out of the room.

Annie looked at Chase, so alone in the barren crib. His face was wet with tears, his little hands reaching out to her. She couldn't leave him, oh, but she had to—for now. As she walked after Dr. Hakim she mentally rehearsed all the facts and figures she'd studied last night on how to raise a healthy baby.

Monroe was waiting for them in what Annie had come to think of as the Michelangelo room. A potted palm tree stood by the window. Annie didn't remember seeing it there before. She wasn't going to waste any time. She had to help Chase fast—he didn't look long for this world.

"Annie." Monroe sat under the painting. "Sit."

Annie sat and was aggravated she'd obeyed so readily. Dr. Hakim sat alongside her. She inched away.

Monroe intertwined his hands in a reverse steeple and stretched his arms, then settled his hands on his lap. "Well, what can I say. Seems we're at a crossroads already. I said it before and I'll say it again. Annie, if you feel like you can't be a part of this team, you best let me know right now."

"Mr. Monroe, I can definitely be a part of the team."

"You're sure?"

"I'm positive, and yesterday, Dr. Hakim…" She turned to him. "…you asked what I was basing my claims on." She held the notebook up. "Now I have the data. All the top hospitals and universities in the country say that for a baby to be healthy it needs a lot of human touch."

Dr. Hakim said nothing and Annie turned back to Monroe, who was ostensibly examining his fingernails.

"So now you're a child-raising expert?" he said. "Are you indeed going to enlighten us?"

She breathed in quickly. "No, it's just that the latest—"

"The latest," Monroe interrupted, "everything is what is sending this world of ours to hell in a hand basket."

Annie gritted her teeth. "Mr. Monroe, the studies all suggest that Chase needs to be picked up when he cries."

"Maat suggests the opposite," Dr. Hakim chipped in.

Oh, forget your Maat, Annie thought. She kept her eyes on Monroe. "They show that the faster a crying baby is picked up, the *less* it cries."

"And real life…" Dr. Hakim again. "…*proves* that babies that are picked up as soon as they cry become little tyrants, little tantrum throwers."

Oh my God, Annie thought. Dr. Hakim sounded so rigid. Monroe was nodding. They couldn't really be serious about this Maat and Isfet stuff, could they? It was beginning to sound like a joke, or like maybe it was a front for something else, but a front for what? Annie remembered holding Chase and his desperate cry for help. He was crying still and crying *like he was dying*. But she realized she wasn't going to win Monroe and Dr. Hakim over with her arguments. It would be counter-productive to even keep trying. No, she'd play along with their Maat nonsense and find another way to help Chase.

"Annie." Monroe was not happy. "I'm going to say it one last time. If you can't be a team player, with Dr. Hakim as the head of the team, you are out."

Annie swallowed hard, nodded and pledged her allegiance.

The rest of the day manifested what her part of the team effort was going to consist of, namely changing Chase's diaper and running out for baby supplies. She was to be basically a servant to Monroe's and Dr. Hakim's whims. She gave what love she could to Chase when she changed him, but except for one time when Dr. Hakim was in the other room, the physical contact she was limited to, as evidenced by Chase's continuous crying, clearly was nowhere near enough. Feedings were non-contact, the formula bottle propped up on a pillow.

Annie had to watch it all and listen to Chase's wailing, tears forming in her own eyes as she looked on helplessly. Yet, she resolved she would find a way to help him. She would.

Crying all the way home that night she formulated a new plan. She instant messaged Tara and set it all up. They would need to meet some contingencies, but if things went their way, tomorrow Chase would get the love he needed. Then she was hoping Monroe and Dr. Hakim would see how well he responded to that love and change their tunes.

* * *

The next day at the compound started off as usual—Dr. Hakim shadowing Annie like a second skin. Monroe was gone though. Annie didn't know where to. She didn't care. The big thing was the plan she'd hatched with Tara could now proceed. She texted Tara to call Dr. Hakim, who took the call right at Chase's crib. Annie could tell what Tara was saying to him based on how he was responding.

"And how, Professor Carey," Dr. Hakim said into his phone, "exactly did you become aware of my work? … I'm flattered, Professor, and of course I'm very familiar with your excellent work as well. …Yes, yes I do have access to a car and what town did you say your symposium was going to be in again?"

*Awesome, Tara*, Annie was thinking. Her friend was pulling the ruse off. Dr. Hakim hung up and explained that he was called away to meet a renowned child psychology professor giving a symposium in Sedona. Annie, feigning concern, asked when Monroe would be back, as she didn't want to be surprised by him popping in. He wasn't expected till late afternoon. Perfect. Dr. Hakim set up a checklist for her on a computer tablet, made sure the formula and supplies were organized and left.

Oh my God. When Annie picked up Chase, his crying ceasing instantly, he glommed on to her so tightly she felt like he was a part of her own body. She talked to him, cooed to him, jiggled him. He clung so fiercely to her she was hesitant to put him back in the crib, so she carried him out to her car with her and one by one brought in the swaddling blankets, the sound machine, the mobiles.

Finally, after a bottle, he relaxed his grip, and she swaddled him in the blankets and laid him down for a nap. While he slept, she put the sound machine on the heartbeat setting and affixed the mobiles to his crib. Oh my God. He slept so peacefully. Motherhood had seemed immaterial to Annie, but now it was clear it was something she was really going to want to do some day. To have another human being so utterly dependent upon her for its existence and well-being was the most powerful thing she'd yet experienced. And the love she'd felt coming from Chase, the most powerful emotion she'd ever felt.

Three men in suits burst into the room. Two white guys, one black. They wore sunglasses. One of the white guys had a tie and long hair.

Annie stood in front of the crib, shielding Chase. "What's going on? Who are you guys?"

"Mr. Monroe sent us," said the long-hair. "Come with us."

Annie squared her shoulders. "I'm watching the baby."

"You disobeyed Mr. Monroe's orders." The long-hair flicked one of the mobiles. "Now come with us."

Every single fiber of Annie's being was saying *Go with him*—the male authority figure compliance syndrome again. But when she looked down at Chase, a wave of protectiveness surged within her. "That's not going to happen."

She'd taken a self-defense class at Alameda. If the long-hair touched her, she'd kick him in the groin. But she wasn't leaving Chase.

They surrounded her. They moved closer. The long-hair said, "You have no choice."

She clenched her fists.

Monroe entered the room. "It's all right. You can go," he said to the men. They left. He walked up to Annie. "What's this?"

"What's what?"

"All this." He yanked the mobiles down.

Annie's heart raced. "I thought they would be nice."

"Where's Dr. Hakim?"

"He got called away."

"Where?"

"I don't know. No, I think he said he was going to Sedona."

Monroe took out his phone and hit a button. He scowled as he waited. "Call me, Hakim." He snapped the phone shut and turned to Annie. "You're gone."

Annie swallowed. "No."

He glared at her. "That's funny. Ha ha. Now get your things and get out."

"You can't fire me."

"I just did."

"No."

"You're good at saying that word. Now out."

Annie told herself to breathe. To just keep breathing. It was Chase that was giving her the courage. "I can make trouble for you."

The side of Monroe's mouth twitched, just a hint of a smirk, as if Annie wasn't worthy of a full one. "I'm going to pretend I didn't hear that."

"I don't want to, but I'm saying I can. I have three thousand Facebook friends and seven thousand Twitter followers."

"So you're threatening me?"

"No." Annie looked him in the eye. "I just want to help Chase."

"Wait a minute. Wait a minute." Monroe ran his hand through his hair. "Let me get this straight. You're threatening to blackmail me and you want me to keep you on?"

"Yes."

# Chapter Five

To Annie's amazement, Monroe had backed down, but he'd also returned Chase to the abysmal conditions as before and kept an even closer watch on Annie. And Annie couldn't help but wonder if he had another reason for letting her stay on as well. Three days passed without incident and now Annie, deeply troubled at how Chase had regressed, was at home on her computer again. She was trying to find Chase's mother. She hoped Chase's mother might be able to get Monroe to improve the level of Chase's care. At the very least, Annie figured Chase's mother would become an ally. She found what she thought was a promising lead.

She told her father she was going to Tara's and armed with only a street address she set out to find Chase's mother. She had to gas up the KIA, the regular trips up and down the mountain to Monroe's burning the fuel. Vivian Sanchez was the name of the woman Annie figured to be Chase's mother. She lived in Glendale, a suburb of Phoenix whose main claim to fame was it had hosted a Super Bowl, but other than that, the city was nothing special. Annie followed the computer's mapping directions into a seedy neighborhood and eventually to a massive apartment building.

The building was seven stories high, many of its windows open, many of the windows with room air conditioners stuck in them, a few with curtains swaying in the dry-heat breeze. Satellite dishes were seemingly everywhere, and chairs, barbecue grills and who knew what else filled the cluttered balconies. Annie's only hope was that Sanchez's name would be on a mailbox in the lobby because she had no apartment number. She looked at the building again. Music blasted from some of the apartments—she could hear it inside the KIA with the windows closed and air conditioning running—some kind of death metal. She was not looking forward to this. She took a deep breath and climbed out.

The lobby had a heavy steel door, tagged with gang signs in magic marker. Annie pulled it open and walked in. A wall of mailboxes to her right, several of the mailbox doors hanging open, some missing altogether, others with fliers stuffed in them, all marked up with gang tagging. On every mailbox door was a little area for a name and apartment number. Most of the information there, if any at all, was taped on little slips of paper.

Three teenage boys, baseball caps askew on their heads, pimp-rolled into the lobby, laughing, jiving, swearing. Annie felt their eyes on her.

One of the boys stepped toward her and said, "Yo, hey pretty mama, was that an earthquake I just felt or are you rocking my world?"

She ignored them but her heart was beating faster. After some aggressive lingering and ogling, the boys left through a door leading into the heart of the building. Annie turned back to the mailboxes and on the third row from the top saw *V. Sanchez: 739*. She looked to the door the boys had just gone through. She felt maybe she ought not to press her luck. Her heart was still leaping in her chest, her breathing quick. Maybe she should just consider it a success she'd found the name and apartment number. She could come back another day for the visit. But her mind kept returning to little Chase. To his sallow face. To the longing in his eyes as Annie—unable to touch him hardly at all—stood helplessly at his crib crying inside. He was wasting away, withering, his spirit calling out to her, *help me, help me*. She walked through the door.

Inside the little room she'd entered, an OUT OF ORDER sign hung on the elevator. Okay, she figured. She'd come this far. She wasn't turning back now.

The stairwell smelled heavily of curry. She didn't want to think about what was on the steps sticking to her sandals. Upward and upward she climbed, cautious at every turn. Finally she was at the seventh floor. She made her way down a hallway, a maroon runner torn up in places and tacked down with a staple gun. The apartment doors were faded, the grain of the wood showing. Near the end of the hall she reached 739. Its door was scratched up and had three locks. She took a deep breath, ran her hands through her hair and knocked.

She saw a shadow behind the peephole, then heard a voice, "Who's there?"

"My name is Annie Rebarchek. I was hoping to speak with Vivian Sanchez."

The light returned to the peephole. A shuffling of deadbolts being slid. The door opened slowly, only a slit. A young, early twenties, Latina in what looked to be a lilac silk blouse and designer jeans asked, "What do you want?"

Annie searched for what to say. As of late, she'd gotten used to deceiving people, but this woman had a kind face and warm brown eyes. Annie decided on honesty. "I was wondering if you were, possibly, Chase Monroe's mother?"

The woman's pretty face tightened, the warmth fled her eyes. She went to shut the door.

"Please!" Annie called. "If you are, Chase is extremely ill. Near death. He's being mistreated by Monroe."

The door opened back up to the slit. "Are you a reporter?"

Annie shook her head.

"If you're not a reporter, just who the hell are you?"

"Monroe hired me to be Chase's nanny."

The woman laughed. "Oh, another one."

"Why, what do you mean?"

The woman smirked. She looked into her apartment and then back at Annie. She opened the door and nodded her in.

Annie's eyes went wide. The apartment didn't match the building. Beautiful wood floors. A mauve sofa with navy throw pillows, an arcing globe lamp dangling over it. Fabulous abstract art work leaned against the walls. An ivory-white bust of some probably famous artist sat atop a pedestal. The apartment was classy and the woman was obviously a painter. "You have a great place."

"You mean especially for this dive apartment building."

"Well, yes, I suppose."

The woman sat in a rust-colored armchair and pointed to the sofa. "So what can I tell you?"

Annie sat. "So." She shrugged. "You're Vivian?"

"I am."

"Well, can you tell me what's going on with your son?"

Vivian laughed.

"Why do you laugh?"

"Oh my." She looked hard at Annie. "How old are you?"

Annie crossed her arms. "Seventeen."

"Seventeen…seventeen. I was seventeen when I nannied for Monroe."

"Really?"

Vivian nodded.

"But—"

Vivian held up a palm. “I know what you’re going to say. I know because I experienced the same thing when I worked for him. Only change is now things are very different for me.” She gazed around the apartment. “Monroe has set me up nicely.”

“That’s not surprising. You being Chase’s mother.”

Vivian laughed again, then caught Annie’s eye. “Look. You seem like a nice kid. And I don’t mean to shock you, but I have to tell you up front before we go any further—if it gets back to Monroe that we talked, you may end up dead.”

Annie gaped at her.

Vivian continued. “Hard to grasp, I know. Listen.” She frowned. “Maybe you just better go. If you’re smart, you’ll say nothing to Monroe about talking to me. This never happened.” She stood. “Good luck to you.”

Annie’s face cringed up. “But Chase. He’s dying.”

Vivian exhaled long and slow and sat back down. “Chase is not my son.”

* * *

Driving home from Vivian Sanchez’s Annie could barely keep her mind on the road. Vivian had sworn her to secrecy three times before she’d laid things out for her. The bottom line? She’d said she was Monroe’s ‘story.’ That when someone got too suspicious of what Monroe was up to with raising a baby alone, she was his reason for having sole custody. She was to play the part of the kid’s mother who had gone to seed, become a meth addict and lived in a run-down tenement building. Monroe was so popular with the media few questioned the story, and those that did feared him too much to pursue it. Vivian never opened her door for the few reporters that dared to show at her apartment.

In exchange, Monroe paid Vivian’s rent, for her art supplies, everything. Chase wasn't her son. He wasn't anyone's. Well, so to speak. She said Monroe was a would-be utopian, pursuing his utopian vision via eugenics, the idea being that he wanted to improve the human race, to breed superior humans, the way ranchers bred prize cattle. Publicly, he was driven to perfect the valley's pollution; privately, to perfect the world's population. At that point, Vivian had shaken her head and said Annie didn't need to know more than that for her own good. Annie had pressed her on who this child psychology professor Dr. Hakim was. Vivian told her Hakim was no such thing. He was a lab worker, forced out of his job at some two-bit college in Tucson for doing unethical experiments on human embryos. Then she'd ushered Annie out of the apartment.

* * *

Monday morning came around quickly. Driving to Monroe's compound, Annie wasn't sure if she still had a job but she was showing up as if she did. Monroe could do what he wanted. For her part she just had to do her best to help Chase. If she didn't, she would have no peace. Speaking with Vivian Sanchez had helped fill in the picture. For what it was worth, Annie figured she'd show up—the compound gate indeed opened without her saying a word when she arrived—and confront Monroe and Dr. Hakim one last time.

She was surprised to find a new member of 'the team' there. As soon as she walked in, Dr. Hakim introduced her to Tanya, supposedly a third-year medical student. Tanya, a pretty, blue-eyed blonde, a bit on the full-figured side, was standing with her hands on her hips. She wore a white medical coat over a gray pinstriped suit.

Monroe wasn't around, confronting him would have to wait,

so Annie went about her business as if nothing were out of the ordinary. It didn't take long to become apparent that Tanya was to replace Dr. Hakim as Annie's shadow, although Dr. Hakim kept popping back in on them too. Annie figured Tanya, with her medical knowledge, was there as well to support Monroe and Dr. Hakim's strange child-rearing theories, which Annie knew now were just a front for the eugenics experiments. Annie went along, did her job, until Dr. Hakim had to take a call and left the room.

Annie figured she had nothing to lose—Chase was looking even worse than on Friday and crying constantly. She walked to Tanya, who was standing with her back to the window in Chase's room, the valley behind her in the distance.

"You realize, Tanya, that what they're doing is making Chase ill."

Tanya abruptly shook her head, her long blonde hair swaying. "I just took Chase's vital signs a few minutes ago. They're within the acceptable range. No, Annie, you're quite mistaken."

"Look at him, Tanya. His skin is yellow. He's grimacing. He never stops crying."

"Babies cry."

"Not like *he* does. He's crying because he's sick. He's crying because he needs love. He's crying…because he's dying."

Monroe walked in, a briefcase under his arm. "Are we having more problems?"

Tanya spoke up. "Annie doesn't seem to think Chase is getting appropriate care. I assured her he is."

"Thank you, Tanya," Monroe said. He turned to Annie. "Annie, get your things and go and don't come back."

* * *

Tears in her eyes Annie kissed Chase and ran from the mansion.

Driving down the mountain she almost hit a pack of bicyclists riding up. She was over-matched by all this. Monroe had too much power. Tanya now would be a witness to Annie's insubordination and would back up Monroe's firing her. A third-year medical student, no one would question her medical knowledge and judgment, especially as opposed to Annie's lack of it. Annie was wedged in, stymied, blocked. All she knew was that she still had to try and help Chase, but if she was going to do that, she was going to have to have help. She headed for the person she trusted more than anyone.

As always, Mrs. Kendall was a willing ear. She welcomed Annie into her cozy apartment. Annie laid it all out for her. She told her everything, ending with being fired—and now not knowing what to do.

Mrs. Kendall agreed Annie was in over her head. She looked her straight in the eye. "I think there's only one thing to do at this point, Annie. You go to the police."

Annie thought about it as she drove home. Going to the police. That would break the whole thing wide open. She thought of how she'd been deceiving her father and now he would know. She thought of how Monroe might retaliate against her. She sighed. Going to the police could be a disaster. But then she thought of Chase.

She would go to the police.

# Chapter Six

Annie drove straight home and pulled into the garage. She checked her face in the KIA's rear view mirror, shut the electric garage door and went inside. Her father was in slippers and sweats—a flex day working from home—in the kitchen making a smoothie in a blender. She bit her lip and waited till the buzz ended.

"Dad."

He turned. "What are you doing home already? Is everything all right?"

"I'm in trouble."

She told him everything. She expected him to hit the ceiling. Instead he changed hurriedly and drove her to the police station.

Detective Rodriguez—clear-eyed, clean-cut, in a shirt and tie with a badge and gun on his belt—asked to speak with Annie alone. Her father sat in a little waiting area.

Detective Rodriguez led Annie to Interview Room #2, a simple room, a wood table surrounded by five chairs. A video camera and monitor sat on the table, the camera lying on its side. The room could've been used for a business meeting, the only things distinguishing it as police-like being the two-way mirror on the wall and a patch of what could've been dried blood on the floor.

Annie told the detective everything.

He asked, "Are you saying you *know* Monroe is intentionally abusing his child?"

"It would appear that way, yes."

"That doesn't answer my question."

"Do I *know?*" Annie thought of Dr. Hakim, of Tanya's medical knowledge, of Monroe's power. Her word against theirs might not amount to much but she had to go for it. "Yes, I know that for an absolute fact."

Detective Rodriguez nodded. "What evidence of the abuse do you have?"

"What evidence?" Annie shrugged. "I have the evidence of what I saw. I told you Chase was yellow, feverish, hoarse from crying constantly."

"But do you have any concrete evidence? Did you take any photos of him? Any video?"

"Well, no, I didn't think to. And then I got fired so suddenly."

"Do you have any experience diagnosing medical conditions?"

Annie didn't like where this was going. "Detective, you're beginning to sound like you're interrogating *me*. Like *I'm* the one who's done something wrong."

He exhaled and gave her what seemed to be a patronizing little smile. "I know it must be hard for you to do what you're doing. At the same time you must realize that much of what *I* do has to do with the difference between what a person remembers as to what the facts are and what the facts actually are. You and I might see the same thing and yet what we say we saw might be substantially different. The questions I'm asking are a way of narrowing down the 'what is said' part to more accurately reflect what actually happened."

Annie nodded but still didn't like the vibe of it all.

He continued. "You do realize Houston Monroe is a major public figure. That all kinds of people say all kinds of things about him, many with ulterior motives."

"Yes, but I'm not one of them, Detective. I know what I know because of what I saw. And I have nothing to gain from any of this."

"All right. Well. It will all be taken into consideration." He shuffled some papers and rose.

"But what about Chase? Are you going to help him?"

"The proper protocols will be followed, as they are in all formal complaints."

"Detective, maybe I didn't express myself well..." She wanted to tell him to sit back down. "...but I'm saying that what Mr. Monroe is doing is *killing* Chase!"

He nodded perfunctorily. "As I said, it will all be taken into consideration."

* * *

"Dad, that detective's not going to do anything," Annie said as her father drove her home from the police station. "I could just tell. He was treating me like some kind of envious fan of Monroe's celebrity."

"Honey, you've done all you could."

Annie was thinking, *have I?* "He was condescending. Implying that *I* was guilty of something. No, nothing good will come of talking to him."

"Well, good or not, honey, it is what it is and quite frankly I'm glad you're out of that whole mess. I really thought Monroe was a stand-up guy. Now I'm not so sure. Who knows what happens to these people when they become so rich. They change."

"So what do I do now?" Annie said as they pulled up the driveway.

"I told you—you've done all you could."

"Dad, that baby is dying!"

He shut the engine and sighed.

*  *  *

Annie wasn't going to wait for the police or anybody else to act. She took to the Internet again and not surprisingly found that both her Twitter and Facebook accounts had been hacked. She knew Monroe must be behind it, but she emailed both companies anyway. Thing was, even if they responded, which was doubtful, it would take days to hear back. Time she couldn't spare.

So she got a list of newspaper reporters in the valley, tracked down their email addresses and started writing them. The messages she wrote evolved with each email, but the basic facts were that baby Chase was being neglected and abused—that he was dying—by billionaire Monroe, and that the police were doing nothing about it.

She expected the replies to pour in but none did. None. Zip. Supposedly the Internet had such power, but she was finding it utterly powerless.

She kept writing though. She wrote reporters in surrounding cities. She wrote and wrote and wrote.

Finally a lone reply popped up in her inbox. From a tiny newspaper at the east end of the valley—the *Superstition Mountain Independent.*

Geez, Annie thought, she herself probably had more followers than the *Superstition Mountain Independent.* She had nothing else though so she called Thaddeus Kostopoulos, the reporter who wrote, and set up a meet.

*  *  *

This was a joke, right? Annie was thinking as she walked into a McDonalds in Mesa. It was him. The reporter. It had to be him. He said he'd be wearing a green and blue striped shirt. He was drinking what looked to be a milkshake and typing on a laptop *and* he looked to be just about her age, okay, maybe a couple of years older but still so young. He had olive skin, dark circles under his eyes, an intense look about him. He was clean-shaven and had a head full of the curliest black hair, nearly an afro.

Annie cleared her throat and walked to him. "Thaddeus?"

He looked up from the laptop and nodded.

"Annie Rebarchek." She put out her hand and they shook.

"Please," he said, sliding the laptop aside. "Have a seat."

She was wondering about him, yes, as she sat, but as Thad—he'd asked her to call him that—asked question after question she became convinced of his sincerity and effectiveness. And his questions, unlike Detective Rodriguez's, were asked in the right spirit, were asked as if he believed what she'd told him.

So Annie felt heard and that was a big relief but still, she couldn't see how an article in the *Superstition Mountain Independent* was going to help Chase in time. "So what do we do?"

Thad pushed some curls off his forehead. "I'm not even considering the print version of the newspaper. Our only chance will be the online edition. This is how I see the scenario playing out: We go to Monroe's, document that the baby is being abused—and that is going to be your responsibility—then break the story online. If we're lucky, the wire services will pick it up, and if we're really lucky, it goes viral. See, the story going viral is everything. If it goes viral, it's like a runaway train that nothing can stop, and although going viral could happen quickly, it almost always takes days or weeks, and from what you've told me, we might not have that long."

"No."

"So, we'll rush everything."

Annie was liking what she was hearing. She might even be liking him. "And how do we do that?"

Thad grimaced. "That's something I'm still in process about. I know the first thing I need to do is get an interview at Monroe's."

Annie smiled a smile that seemed to say, 'And you think you'll be able to do that working for the *Superstition Mountain Independent?*'

He nodded, as if catching her drift. "Monroe might not want an interview with the *Independent* but he will with CNN, which wants to interview him about his crusade to clear up the valley's air pollution."

"Okay, but how will you pull that off?"

"I'll lie."

She laughed.

"Well, the baby's life is on the line. I'll do whatever it takes."

"Yes." Annie nodded. "And what will I do?"

"You'll be my assistant."

"Okay, but Monroe's not going to let me within a hundred yards of his place."

"Well, I wouldn't be telling him who you were. You'd be Miranda Elliot."

She crinkled her nose. "Who?"

"That's the name on an extra press pass I have. You would just have to be in the background. I have a friend who's a makeup artist. Once she gets done with you, they'll never recognize you. The only thing you'll have to be mindful of is your voice. Just don't say anything if you can help it, and nod if introduced."

Annie was figuring she could do it. She was figuring she

could do anything to save Chase—and it was feeling awfully good to have someone like Thad helping her.

# Chapter Seven

The next morning Annie was sitting in a chair being turned into a different person. She was at Thad's friend's, the makeup artist, getting longer eyelashes, black contacts over her brown eyes, a blonde wig over her brown hair, and a prosthetic nose. Amazing, she thought as she watched the transformation. *She* didn't recognize herself any more. She felt confident no one else would either.

Thad, or Max Orlov, his assumed CNN name, had pulled off getting the interview with Monroe at his mansion, and now that the makeup artist was done they headed there. Annie was to be Thad's assistant, Miranda Elliot. I'm Miranda Elliot, she was thinking as she pinned on the press pass Thad gave her. I'm Miranda Elliot. Oh well, this ought to be interesting.

Thad showed his press pass to the video camera at the compound gate. "Max Orlov. CNN." The mechanized, heavy steel gate swung slowly open. He rolled up his window, the air conditioning in his Mazda running hard in the heat. He turned to Annie. "You okay, *Miranda?*"

"Sure," she said. She took a deep breath. "Before we get there, though, *Max,* I want to tell you how grateful I am for you taking this on with me."

He nodded and drove up the drive.

Annie had a brief thought of what her father would have to say about what she was doing. She was flagrantly disrespecting his wishes *again*. But on second thought maybe that was a good thing. Maybe this is what she needed to do to honor her promise to her mother to break free from subservience to male authority.

Anyway, ultimately this was all about Chase. The Mazda cruised to a halt in front of the double doors. She and Thad exchanged a look and climbed out.

Thad tossed her the car keys and she opened the trunk and grabbed the camera pack and lighting tripod. He had shown her how to set everything up. There was really nothing for her to say to Monroe or anybody else. Just nod if she was introduced.

Dr. Hakim, bubbling over with enthusiasm, met them at the door. He led them across the mansion, Annie hearing Chase crying in the distance, to the Michelangelo room, where Monroe was sitting on the sofa. Monroe was dressed in a white suit, and even wore white loafers and a white tie. He stood quickly and shook hands with Thad. Then he stepped to Annie and offered his hand. Annie shook, nodded and looked him squarely in the eye. Anything less would be a tip-off something was off-kilter. Monroe reacted normally, she thought. Hmm, this just might work.

She set up the camera, tripod and spotlight, trying to look professional, but all the while she was alarmed by Chase's woeful crying. It sounded as if he was even worse, his cry weakened, wizened. Even if all went according to plan of Thad's story being picked up by the wires and going viral it still might be too late to save him.

The interview proceeded, Thad asking intelligent, informed questions about the phenomenal success of Monroe's waste removal company, Green Magic—over three million customers in metropolitan Phoenix alone—and about his plans to clean up the valley's 'brown cloud' of air pollution. Monroe replied equally intelligently and informatively. Annie was thinking Monroe *was* an impressive person. If only it weren't for what he was doing to

Chase, she would've liked him. But Chase's sad crying wiped out that feeling entirely.

The interview went on. Annie was sweating from the heat of the spotlight. Monroe and Thad were in the camera's viewfinder and she was recording them, but the heat of the spotlight was so intense she had to move her face away. Dr. Hakim hung at the edge of things, smiling, an interested observer. Annie was grateful he didn't say anything to her. She just kept telling herself to nod if he did. Maybe he would think she was mute. Finally, his cell rang and he hurried off to take the call.

Annie could sense the interview winding down. Thad had Monroe smiling, laughing, puffing out his chest like he was the Master of the Universe, but Thad was also running out of questions—and Annie was running out of time to get the evidence of Chase's being abused.

Tanya, the third-year medical student, approached, perhaps drawn by the hubbub, still in the white lab coat, her blonde hair long down her back. Oh no, Annie thought, she was coming closer. Tanya smiled and Annie nodded. The heat from the spotlight was so intense and Annie was sweating so, that the heavy makeup Thad's stylist friend had applied started drifting down her forehead and into her eyes. She wiped her eyes as Tanya sidled up to her.

Just don't say anything to me, Annie was thinking. Her eyes started stinging from the makeup and she kept rubbing them.

Tanya leaned close and said softly, "You okay?"

Annie nodded but still wiped at her eyes. Just go away, she was thinking. But hearing Chase continuing to cry it was as if something hit her, as if something formulated in her mind. She looked in the camera viewfinder and then back at Tanya. In her deepest guttural voice she whispered to Tanya, "Watch this for me for a second?"

"You got it."

Annie hurried off—eyes still burning but determined to do her part—straight to Chase. Oh, he looked terrible. She snapped several pics with her phone, and broader shots to show that Chase was in Monroe's mansion. Then she caught some video as well—she wanted the audio of him crying. She stuffed the phone into her pocket and picked up Chase. He was a wraith, just a slip of himself. And there was no clinging to her this time. It was as if his spirit had been broken, as if he'd given up. He cried weakly and Annie started crying too, but then she became so angry at Monroe and Dr. Hakim for what they were doing to him.

Oh. These men. These men were killing this poor baby. She could hear the interview ending. They were killing him and she hadn't been able to help. And, yes, who knew how long it would take for Thad's story to go viral, if it ever did, and who even knew if the story going viral would be enough? Monroe had so much money and was such a media darling, he seemingly had the power to stop anything they might try.

She could hear Thad thanking Monroe for the interview. This was it. Tanya and Dr. Hakim would come looking for her any second. She had Chase in her arms right here and right now. For this instant, she could keep him safe. For this instant, she could protect him. But soon that would all change, unless…

She had Thad's car keys. Chase finally stopped crying. She kissed him. She could race Chase to the police station where they would *have to* investigate Monroe's abuse. It would be a crazy risk, but it was a crazy situation. Annie remembered a saying her mother always used to tell her: 'Desperate situations call for drastic measures.'

She kissed Chase again and with him in her arms headed for the door. She tip-toed by the Michelangelo room, feeling the heat of the spotlight even from a distance, hoping against hope she wouldn't be noticed. So far so good. She went through the mansion's various rooms, trying desperately to remember which way led to the double doors and Thad's Mazda. She turned a corner and Dr. Hakim was coming up a flight of marble steps.

Dr. Hakim smiled but when he realized Chase was in her arms his smile faded. "What are you doing?"

Annie pushed him down the steps, his long hair flailing as he tumbled backward. She heard him moaning as she ran down the steps and to the double doors. Come on, come on, hurry, she told herself as she undid the deadbolt and tried to remember the code for the alarm system. 7211, no, 7217. Ah screw it. She yanked open the door and a blaring alarm sounded. Searchlights criss-crossed the parking lot even though it was midday. Annie just focused on what she had to do. She dug Thad's car keys out of her pocket and opened the Mazda's door. She set Chase on the seat, hopped in, tucked him in next to her side and buckled them both in with her seat belt.

She turned the ignition as Dr. Hakim burst out of the mansion. She popped the doors locked. Dr. Hakim pounded on her window with his fists. He was yelling something in a foreign language. Chase started crying. Annie put the car in reverse and backed, Dr. Hakim running along with her, pounding and yelling. When she had enough room to turn around she braked and popped the car into drive. Dr. Hakim jumped onto the hood and scrambled up onto the windshield. Oh, she couldn't see anything but the sides of the road. She accelerated and then hit the brakes.

Dr. Hakim slid down the hood but was right in front of the car. She would've had to run him over to keep going. He climbed back onto the windshield.

"Get off!"

He didn't budge. He was laughing. In the rear view mirror Annie saw people running out of the double doors to vehicles in the lot. She shook her head and hit the gas. "Fine," she said. "You wanna stay there, stay there." She trusted that she was in the middle of the road by what she could see in her peripheral vision and down the long drive the Mazda headed for the compound gate.

Annie considered stopping but the vehicles were following now. She held Chase close to her hip. "Hang on, baby!"

The Mazda smashed through the gate, Dr. Hakim yelling and getting swept up the windshield, over the roof and tumbling onto the drive behind. Annie glanced in the rear view mirror. The vehicles chasing had to stop in order to not run over Dr. Hakim.

Now, how to get to the police station? Her sense of direction was oriented from her house in the valley. She raced down the mountain switchback road, hanging on to Chase during the turns. Remarkably enough he'd stopped crying. That was it—Annie remembered. The police station was in downtown Phoenix. She'd take the Black Canyon Freeway and exit Van Buren or Jefferson.

She got on the Freeway. The Mazda had decent acceleration, but a white Jaguar raced up behind her like she was standing still. It came up alongside. Monroe. He motioned for her to pull over.

Not going to happen, Bucko, Annie thought and she put the pedal to the floor. It would only be five minutes until she was at the police station. Monroe could follow her there for all she cared, and once they got there, it would be all over, and then the media would have to find out about Monroe's abuse. Chase would be saved.

Her phone rang. She would have a hard time answering it now. She whizzed past an oil refinery truck. Again, Monroe pulled alongside. He was honking. The phone only had one more ring before it went to messages. She snatched it from her purse. "Yeah?"

"Annie, it's Thad. You okay?"

She nodded. "Yes. Are you? I'm sorry. I didn't mean to leave you like that."

"You have the baby? Where you going?"

She swung behind an eighteen wheeler to get away from Monroe. She took a quick breath. "Yeah, I've got him and I'm going to the police station. Once I get there I'm just going to lay on the horn till the cops come out."

"Bad idea."

Her heart sank. She had no Plan B. "Why?"

"The sheriff is corrupt. He's in Monroe's back pocket."

"Oh God. So what do I do? I've got Monroe on my tail."

"Can you lose him?"

She shook her head. "He's got this super-fast car." Annie saw the interchange for I10 coming up. "Wait." She threw the phone down onto the seat and swung all the way over to the far left lane, waited for Monroe to follow suit, then floored the Mazda and swerved in front of a garbage truck and cut back across all the lanes and exited I10. She grabbed the phone. "Oh my God."

"What?"

"I think I just lost him."

"Great. So where are you now?"

"On I10."

"Which way you going?"

"Wait a second. Let me check. Uh…east."

"Okay, that's perfect. Now just stay on I10 until you get to U.S. Route 60. Then take that. 60 is the Superstition Freeway."

"I know. I know it. My dad used to take me out to Canyon Lake on it when I was little."

"Canyon Lake. Okay. Then you know where the steamboat ride is there?"

"Yes." She removed the blonde wig and the nose prosthesis and tossed them into the back seat. She took a good long breath through her nose.

"Go there. Park in a far corner of the lot, back into a spot so no one can see the rear license plate. There's no plate on the front. I'll meet you there."

Annie looked at Chase and sighed. Her plan to drive to the police station had been comforting, but now that she remembered how condescending Detective Rodriguez had been when she'd sought his help, maybe staying away from the police was the right move. She hardly knew Thad but he'd already taken a big risk on Chase's behalf. She felt she could trust him. She nodded. "I'll be there."

* * *

Annie saw a department store from the highway and went in for baby supplies and a car seat for Chase. Her mind wandered while she waited in line at the check-out with Chase asleep in her arms. She realized in the eyes of the law she was doing something very wrong. Oh, it was *morally* right but she was sure that legally the charges would be abduction or kidnapping. On top of that she'd read about the sheriff being nasty—and if Monroe had him in his back pocket like Thad said…

"Baby fast asleep," an Asian American man behind her in line said. "What's your baby's name?"

Annie smiled. *Her* baby! She didn't want to say *Chase*. She looked at the cart a young couple had in front of her. The stuffed cart had a package of hot dogs on top. "Frank," Annie said. "My baby's name is Frank."

"Frank good name." The man nodded.

Back on the road again, Annie realized she wasn't accustomed to the winding, steep, cliff-edged road that had to be taken to get to Canyon Lake. It would've been scary enough on her own but being responsible for Chase amped up her anxiety level. Only when she hit the rare flat stretch was she able to check on Chase and then glance at the deep purple lake cut into the middle of golden sheer-faced mountain cliffs. "Beautiful," she said and she prepared for another tough stretch.

Chase woke as she pulled into the steamboat ride's parking lot. She backed into a spot in the far corner as Thad had suggested and gave Chase his bottle. She was relieved and gratified to see him eat. Earlier at Monroe's, he'd seemed beyond reaching, like a dog that had been beat too much.

After his bottle she changed him and set him down in swaddling blankets on the backseat for a nap. She laughed. She needed a nap too. All the drama had sucked the energy out of her.

A taxi rolled into the lot and Thad, unmistakable in his bushy black hair, jumped out. Annie found herself smiling as he walked to the Mazda. He climbed in the passenger side.

"You okay?" he asked.

She nodded. "You?"

"And the baby?"

She shrugged. "As good as can be I suppose. At least now he

has a chance."

Thad looked at Chase. "He seems okay."

She laughed. "A bit of a basic assessment, but all right."

He smiled.

"Thad," she said. She liked the name. She waved her phone in front of him. "I've got photos of Chase in his crib at Monroe's. We've got our documentation of the abuse."

"Excellent."

She was feeling good being with him. He was so sincere. So clean somehow. She gazed at him and they inadvertently caught eyes. She quickly looked away, and up on the winding road two police cruisers were making their way toward the steamboat parking lot. "Looks like we've got company."

Thad looked.

"So what are we going to do now?" she asked.

"Uh...my office isn't far from here but I didn't plan on the police showing up." He waited. "What do you think we should do?"

She liked that he asked her opinion. She checked the steamboat's schedule sign. It was leaving in three minutes. "Let's go on a boat ride."

"Good idea." He glanced at the cops. "Yeah."

Annie handed Thad the baby bag she'd bought, leaned over the console and gently gathered Chase in her arms. "Okay, little man." She turned to Thad. "I think I'm good."

Thad shook his head. "Throw the wig and the nose prosthesis in the bag."

"Why?"

"Because they're looking for a blonde with a big nose named Miranda Elliot. Not a..." His eyes lingered on hers. "...pretty brunette with a cute little nose."

Annie breathed in deep and felt a tingling in her neck. She felt she might be blushing.

Thad ran for the steamboat and got them to hold off departing until Annie walked over with Chase. The three of them crossed the iron walkway onto the steamboat, the attendant pulling up the ramp just as the police cruisers barreled into the parking lot.

"Well," Thad said as he took Annie's hand and led her through the people to the front of the steamboat. "We bought ourselves a little time anyway. How long does this take? Do you remember?"

"Ninety minutes."

"Ninety minutes, okay."

Mountain vistas opened up before them. It was cooler on the boat, a breeze spreading across the water. That this lake, Annie was thinking, existed in the middle of these mountains seemed a miracle, and it seemed they'd be needing a miracle to get out of the jam they were in. She gazed at Chase, sleeping peacefully in her arms. He didn't seem worried in the least. She turned to Thad. "It is beautiful out here."

He bit his lip and nodded. "It's an amazing land."

"Look! Isn't that a bald eagle?"

The majestic bird soared along a golden sheer cliff.

"Yeah, yeah," he said. "It sure is."

The steamboat turned and Annie saw the police cruisers at the dock. Undoubtedly they'd seen Thad's Mazda. She frowned. The boat approached the cliff the eagle had soared along. Up close the cliff was towering, tremendous. "So." She nodded toward the cruisers. "Any ideas?"

He winked at her. "Swim for it?"

Thad had a worldly experience in his countenance, like a person who'd gotten through tight spots before and wasn't intimidated when he found himself in new ones. Yeah, she was liking being with him. She was liking it very much. "I didn't buy those little inflatable arms for Chase."

He laughed. Then his face went into complete concentration. He said nothing, the breeze blowing the curls off his forehead. He searched the people on the steamboat.

Annie waited.

He turned to her. "Do you have anything sharp in the baby bag?"

She thought. "I bought a pair of scissors at the store to trim Chase's nails."

"Give them to me."

She did and he took off, disappearing below deck.

A couple of minutes later he returned with short, very short hair.

"Oh my God," Annie said. "Talk about a complete makeover."

He shrugged. "Annie, the cops are looking for a couple—a blonde woman with a big nose and a guy with bushy black hair. So we split up and leave the boat separately. Then there's five babies on-board, two with blonde mothers. The cops I'm sure know my name from running the plates on the Mazda so if I get stopped when I deboard I'm screwed, but you have a very good shot of making it by them."

Annie smiled. Thad was so confident, so cool and smart.

Chase gurgled. Annie laughed and gazed at him. "And you! You they will never recognize, right, Frank?"

"Frank?"

"His new name."

"See you and Frank in the parking lot." Thad drifted into the people.

The boat pulled up to the dock.

Annie took a deep breath. She was just a young single mom on a boat ride with her baby, that was all, she told herself. Wearing blade sunglasses and scowls in the late afternoon sun, the cops stood like sentries, like bouncers at a bar, on the sides of the iron walkway as it clanked onto the concrete landing.

The departing passengers eyed the cops curiously. One by one they went by like sheep to the slaughter. None were stopped until a blonde woman with a baby was asked to step to the side. Not good, Annie thought, and she would soon be next.

She was sure the cops behind their mirrored sunglasses could see right through her. They knew she was no mother. She was a seventeen-year-old high school kid. She almost stopped when she got to them but walked on and they let her pass. She cradled Chase and drifted along with the crowd until it was safe to turn and look for Thad.

He was the last one to deboard. He was so cool-looking, so carefree, so poised. She was proud of him. Of his courage, his cool.

The cops stopped him.

She wanted to go to him but knew it wouldn't help. So far they were just talking to him. If Thad pulled his wallet to show I.D. he'd be sunk. Now the cops were smiling, laughing, and Thad laughed too and walked off.

Annie played it nonchalant, walking along the cars in the parking lot as if looking for hers. The sun was still powerful even this late in the day and she was careful to keep Chase's little face out of it. Now here came Thad. "What happened with the cops, Thad?"

"I followed the old 'best defense is an offense' theory—*I* stopped to talk to *them*."

"And what did you say?"

"I asked them why they were there."

"And what did they say?"

"That they were looking for us." He laughed. "No, they said they were looking for suspects in a kidnapping."

Annie swallowed. "So they *were* looking for us?"

"Well, yeah."

Annie's heart pounded. Kidnapping was so serious. She wondered how Thad was able to stay so cool about it all. "And why were they laughing?"

"Because I told them a joke."

She laughed.

But now they were still in danger. No car. Cops after them as *kidnappers*. Monroe after them too. Annie sighed. "We really need to get out of here."

"Uh-huh. The *Independent's* office is in Apache Junction, just a half hour from here. By car, that is. Once we get there there's an old souped-up beater we can use."

Annie smiled. "Maybe you could ask your cop friends to give us a lift?"

He laughed, all the while looking around intently.

"I've got it." Annie touched his elbow. "Leave this one to me."

# Chapter Eight

Annie told a kindly-looking older couple that their car broke down and they needed a lift. Seeing Chase, the couple had readily agreed and driven them to a couple of blocks from—Thad didn't want to be dropped off right in front—the *Superstition Mountain Independent* office.

Apache Junction was an old-time Arizona town, and Annie felt good walking down its quiet streets, homes with rock gardens instead of lawns, the brute sheer-faced cliffs of Superstition Mountain looming over their shoulders. And it felt good to walk with Thad and Chase. It was crazy maybe but Annie was fantasizing, just for a moment, that the three of them were a family. Yeah, it felt really good.

Thad insisted they keep walking until he became convinced there were no police at the *Independent*. Finally they went for it. The office was nothing special, just on the end of a little strip mall. A grainy ancient sign, faded pink walls, an overhang atop a boardwalk. Real estate listings, fliers for community events were taped to the plate-glass windows. Off to the side sat a lone newspaper box filled with the *Superstition Mountain Independent*. Annie smiled and said, "Looks like the big-time to me."

Thad smiled back. "Don't laugh. When a hot story breaks on the Internet it doesn't matter where it comes from." He slipped his key into the lock and opened the door.

The office was wood paneled with three big desks with in/out wire baskets on them. A cork bulletin board, filled with 3x5 cards scribbled over with notes, was nailed to one of the walls. Huge, bound packs of newspapers sat on the floor near the door. Annie kept gazing around. Her eyes landed on a couple of framed black and white photos. They were of the office back in the day. Instead of plaster board the original office walls had been horizontal wood strips. Not quite a log cabin but not far from it either. The street out front was dirt. There were hitching posts and horses tied to them. The ancient sign alone was the same. "This was really how it looked?"

Thad nodded. He booted up a computer. "Back then Apache Junction *was* the Wild West. Prospectors flooded the area mining and panning for gold. Saloons, cowboys, gunslingers, the whole deal."

"What do you think of that, Chase?" Annie said, jiggling him on her hip.

"Oh, this doesn't look good," Thad said, glued to the monitor.

Annie shivered. She didn't like the fear in his voice. "What doesn't?"

"Monroe has mobilized the entire valley to find Chase. He's got Sheriff 'Hang 'Em' Hank Delgado on TV railing already." He turned to her. "Annie." He shook his head. "They're going to know who I am from the Mazda's plates. I'm no good to you now."

"What? Wait a minute." She clutched Chase tighter. "I mean, I'm sorry I got you into this and all, but I hope you're not going to bail on us now."

He shook his head again. "It's not a question of bailing." He jumped up and walked to the front window. He opened a desk drawer and rummaged until he found a screwdriver. "Stay here."

"Where are you going?"

He slipped out the door.

Annie checked the monitor. "Oh my God," she said, holding

Chase close. The man on the screen looked so bitter. Gray hair sticking out from his Smokey the Bear sheriff hat, glasses, and his face had a permanent scowl on it, an anger furrow an inch wide on his forehead. The headline: HANG 'EM HANK CALLS FOR DEATH PENALTY FOR KIDNAPPERS.

Annie scrolled down to a photo of Monroe and another headline: VALLEY PHILANTHROPIST OFFERS TEN MILLION DOLLAR REWARD FOR BRINGING IN BABY STEALERS.

When the office door opened Annie jumped. Chase cried. Not for long though. Maybe, Annie thought, he'd sensed her alarm. She resolved to stay calm. Thad was carrying a New Mexico license plate.

"So you saw?" he said.

Annie nodded.

He walked hurriedly by. "Lock the front door and pull the shades."

"Why? What's going on?"

"Just do it."

She obeyed. It was the old knee-jerk obedience to male authority again, but coming from Thad it especially hurt.

He went out a back exit and when he returned he said, "Okay, it's ready."

"What is?"

"The beater. The car you can use. It's an old souped-up V-8 Chevy that hasn't been registered."

"Thad, please tell me what's going on."

"Annie." He sat at the computer and sighed. "They know who I am from running the plates on the Mazda. The *only* chance you have now is going it alone."

"No."

"Trust me, it is. With facial recognition technology and the video surveillance Sheriff Delgado has all over the valley I'll be a sitting duck. You, on the other hand, they don't know who you are yet."

She took a deep breath.

"You can do it. But you've got to act fast. Do you have a credit card?"

"My father's."

"Give it to me. Do you have any relatives out of state?"

She handed him the card. She swallowed and said, "An aunt living in Seattle."

He typed an airline website into the address bar and brought up the schedule of flights to Seattle.

"What are you doing?"

He chose a flight and entered the credit card information.

"Thad, what are you doing?"

"Buying you time."

"But I'm not going to Seattle."

"The police will think you are."

"But what happens when I don't get on the plane?"

"They'll think you went another way."

Annie nodded.

"Okay." The transaction complete, he turned to her. "Here's what you're going to do. Go to every ATM you see and max out on the cash you can get, then toss the credit card in the trash."

"All right."

"Hang on to your phone for the photos. Annie, those photos are everything. Everything! If you lose them, it's all over. If you need to make a call, buy a disposable prepaid cell. After the call toss the phone and then get the hell out of there."

"Thad—"

"If you need to use the Internet, use it only from a library or from somebody else's phone or computer. If you have to use it from your phone, make sure you're driving."

"Thad—"

"Keep wearing the black contacts and go to a beauty shop where no one knows you and get your hair cut and dyed red."

"Thad—"

"Zero contact with anyone from your past."

"Thad, stop."

He did.

"What will *you* do?"

A pounding on the front door.

Thad jumped up and said softly, "I'll be okay. Now the car is idling behind the building. Go."

More pounding.

Annie grabbed the baby bag and ran out the back.

* * *

Annie held Chase close to her hip as she pulled away from the *Superstition Mountain Independent* office in the souped-up Chevy beater. "We're going to have to get this done somehow, little man, but we can do it, right?" she said. She stopped at a red light. A police cruiser pulled up next to her. She told herself to just keep looking straight ahead. Just keep looking straight ahead.

The light turned and she pulled away, feeling the surge of the old Chevy's power in her gut. She kept an eye on the cruiser in her rear view mirror and checked for a speed limit sign. Okay. Thirty-five. She was cool. And wow, this car had some juice. Not like the KIA. It was old, yes, but it was a powerhouse.

Chase needed his bottle but first she mentally went over all the things Thad had told her. They made sense and she could do them, but still it seemed the odds were stacked so high against them. The one thing she resolved that was their ace in the hole though was the truth. The truth was on their side. That was something Monroe and Sheriff Delgado and his deputies and the whole wide world couldn't change. Monroe had been abusing Chase. And now she had the photos to prove it and she was going to let the world know. But first—she saw a bank with a drive-through ATM and turned into its parking lot—she had to take care of the things Thad had told her to buy them time.

* * *

The truth. The truth. That was all Annie could think about as she sat in the beautician's chair at the Salamander Beauty Salon in Justiceburg, way outside Phoenix's city limits, the red hair dye stinging the back of her neck. It was early the next morning—she figured there'd be less people then—and she was yawning. She had to keep herself and Chase free until she got the photos of Monroe abusing him out there. That was her sole mission. Keep it simple, she told herself.

The dye job over, she looked in the mirror as the stylist raised her hair gently in her hands to display the color.

"You like?" The stylist peered carefully at her in the mirror too. She had caring gray eyes, her simply styled black hair in a pretty bob. "If you don't, I can change it. Lighter, darker, frosted, tipped, just let me know."

Annie looked back at Chase, two of the women in the beauty shop volunteering to watch him. He was continuing his recovery bit by bit. More responsive. Eating more. Sleeping better. It seemed the better Annie felt, the better he did too, and vice-versa, like they were developing a symbiotic relationship of mother and child.

Annie had done her best to follow Thad's instruction of 'zero contact' with anyone from her past. It had been hard but she'd answered no calls, listened to no voice mails, checked no emails or texts. She'd run into Walmart to buy Chase supplies and another car seat but that was it. She missed being able to talk to Tara and desperately wished she could get advice from her father and Mrs. Kendall, but so far she'd been able to hold the line. She'd loved talking to Chase but felt the need for contact with someone more her own age too. The stylist seemed so nice. "I think I want to have it cut too."

The stylist put her hands on her hips, comb and brush held at wide angles. "Well, you're going to change just about everything now, aren't you?"

The question could've been threatening but the stylist's tone was friendly.

"You know, Justiceburg is such a small town," she said, "and I've never seen you before. I really should rightly introduce myself. My name is Beatrice Parker."

Beatrice's southwestern formality of phrase reminded Annie of Stu, the Texan, Tara's friend from Alameda High.

"An—" Annie started to say *Annie* but thinking to keep up her false identity cut her name off mid syllable.

"Ann." Beatrice nodded and twirled the comb in her hand.

Annie shook her head. "It's actually Andrea."

"Well, very nice to meet you, actually Andrea." She put the comb in her pocket and the two shook hands.

Beatrice was cutting Annie's hair. No one seemed to be waiting for Beatrice, so the stylist was taking her time, making small talk, chatter really, which Annie was enjoying until Beatrice said:

"So, hon, what brings you and baby to Justiceburg?"

Annie didn't have a story rehearsed. "Uh."

"Oh, that's okay. You have to excuse me and my god-awful nosiness, always butting into other people's business."

Annie felt like she had to say something. "I had some trouble with baby Frank's father."

"Ah."

"He had anger management issues."

Beatrice blew the bangs off her forehead. "Oh, honey, I can't tell you how much I can relate to that. I've got stories to tell about my ex that would never end."

Annie paid in cash. Everything in cash, like Thad said. She really wouldn't have minded meeting with Beatrice afterward for coffee, but she was just too unsure of anything at this point.

When she got in the Chevy, she looked at herself in the rear view mirror, at her short-ish red hair. "Who are you?" she asked. She looked at Chase. "Do you still recognize me?"

Feeling there was no time to waste, she drove to the Justiceburg Public Library. With seemingly everyone in the valley after them, she had to act fast.

Annie asked the librarian, a woman with gray hair and glasses and a vest filled with buttons, including a "I Love Justiceburg" one, if she could use an Internet terminal.

She could. The librarian gave her a pass and pointed her toward two terminals on the far side of the room. "Use terminal two. They're marked with masking tape on the sides."

Annie figured this was the least risky of things to try and she figured the Internet was how she'd found Thad so it was worth a shot. She headed to the terminals and settled in with Chase on her lap at terminal two.

"Baby baby," she cooed, gazing into his little blue eyes, looking up so lovingly at her. Okay now, she told herself, she needed to get cutting. First off, she checked news sites to see if she could find anything about Thad. No luck. Then she brought up a list of newspaper and TV reporters' email addresses—ones she hadn't written to before—and proceeded to write down a cross section of them, twenty total. Chase was getting fidgety, and she didn't want to draw undue attention or push her luck, so she packed him up and headed back out to the Chevy.

Chase safely in the car seat next to her, they were leaving the library lot when a police cruiser pulled in. He couldn't be there for her, could he? There was no way he could've known. No, she told herself. It was just a coincidence. She didn't want to start getting paranoid. Still, one way or another, she figured it was time to be moving on. She drove to the motel, packed up their things and left.

# Chapter Nine

Where to go next? Annie figured since the police could track them wherever they went, they'd be as safe in Phoenix as anywhere else, and as Thad had said—the best defense was an offense. No one would expect them to return to Sheriff 'Hang 'em' Hank Delgado's backyard. At least she hoped they wouldn't. The key thing was to keep moving.

On the drive back to Phoenix she sent the emails, along with the photos and video of Chase, to the TV and newspaper reporters. It was a juggling act—she drove slow and was extra careful—but she got it done. There, she thought. Now things were going to turn their way. All she had to do until then was keep Chase and herself free.

In the meantime it would really help to get some advice. That meant Mrs. Kendall. Annie knew what Thad had said about no contact with anyone from her past, but if Annie trusted anybody in the world it was Mrs. Kendall. Annie bought a prepaid cell phone and called to see if she could stop by. She could. She tossed the cell and drove there.

After a bottle, Chase had fallen asleep and Annie carried him carefully, shielding his face from the scorching afternoon sun, to Mrs. Kendall's door. Mrs. Kendall welcomed them but her normally peaceful countenance wasn't there—she seemed troubled—and she didn't say anything about the baby or Annie's new hair color and cut. Oh well, Annie figured Mrs. Kendall probably had problems of her own, and Annie felt guilty about always coming to her with hers. Always taking and never giving.

Mrs. Kendall's apartment was as usual calming. Annie could

feel its beauty soothing her soul as she settled the sleeping Chase in between two throw pillows on the sofa. Now, she figured, maybe she could give a little something back. She sat next to Chase and said, “Mrs. Kendall, is everything all right with you? Is there anything *you* need to talk about?”

“I was going to ask you the same thing, Annie.” The pretty woman didn’t sit, choosing instead to pace back and forth.

Annie, dying to unburden herself, started telling her what she and Chase had been going through, but no sooner did she begin when Mrs. Kendall held up a palm.

Annie shrugged. What?

“I know the whole story, Annie. I’ve been following it on the TV news.”

Annie’s stomach churned. Mrs. Kendall’s tone was harsh, accusative. “But you haven’t heard my side of the story. You haven’t got the truth.”

Mrs. Kendall stopped pacing and drilled Annie with a look. “The *truth* is that you stole a baby.”

Annie felt her heart stop beating. She couldn’t breathe. She looked at Chase, then back at Mrs. Kendall. “But I was beginning to tell you *why* I took him. About the abusive things Monroe was doing—”

“Annie, in this case whatever reasons you might have are trumped by the fact that you stole his baby.”

She kept saying *stole*, Annie thought. “That’s not fair, Mrs. Kendall, and if you’d let me finish—”

“Annie.” Mrs. Kendall took a step toward her. “I love you like a second daughter, you know that, but in this instance there is just no gray. To steal—”

“I didn’t *steal* him.”

Mrs. Kendall pulled a cell phone from her pocket. "There's only one thing to do." Her tone was unbending. "You need to call the police and turn yourself in."

Annie nearly fainted. She stood. "No. Mrs. Kendall, please, you weren't listening to me—Chase was *dying*."

"And so now is his father. In fact, you're the one killing him." She thrust Annie the phone. "Call. Now."

Annie looked at Chase. She remembered Monroe's eugenics. Dr. Hakim's weird Maat philosophy. Chase lying there abandoned, shriveling up, crying, dying. "I won't."

Mrs. Kendall frowned. "Then I will." She started putting in the number.

Annie rose and stepped toward her. She reached for the phone but Mrs. Kendall with longer arms held her off. Meanwhile, the commotion set Chase to crying.

"Hello," Mrs. Kendall said into the phone. "I'm at 4281 Cherry Lane in Phoenix."

Annie pushed Mrs. Kendall hard and she fell back into an armchair. "Oh!" she cried.

Annie grabbed the phone and hung up. "You didn't listen to me, Mrs. Kendall! You just didn't listen!"

* * *

Annie gathered up Chase and ran from Mrs. Kendall's apartment. What had been going on back there? she wondered as she fumbled the Chevy's key into the ignition. Chase was wailing from the car seat next to her. "Chase! Please stop! I can't think!" The police would be on the scene in a flash.

Annie put her foot down on the gas and the Chevy tore off. Camp Lake Choctaw, she was thinking, or more likely the thought had already been floating through her brain. Camp Lake

Choctaw…Camp Lake Choctaw…Camp Lake Choctaw, the summer day camp where Tara worked. She headed for it. The sun was low in the sky and nearly blinding as she drove straight west. She had the visor down and her hand in front of her face but still, it was like driving into a cloud. Thoughts whirled around her brain. Mrs. Kendall had turned on her. Seemed like everyone was.

She stopped at a light. On the corner sat a newspaper box. Her photo—her junior yearbook photo—stared back at her. The headline: BABY SNATCHER VIGILANTE POSSE GROWS.

Well, there you go, she thought. The cat was finally fully out of the bag. Then she remembered she had the short red hair and the black contacts, but even so, her face was her face, and also Mrs. Kendall would probably tell the police about her new appearance. Whatever though. She drew in a deep breath. It was what it was. She'd deal with it.

At least Chase had stopped crying. It was funny but she felt what it must feel like for parents to love their kids and still be incredibly frustrated with them. She stroked his cheek.

The light turned and she laughed. At least she couldn't say it was a boring summer. And she kept telling herself that they had the truth on their side and that when the truth came out—when the public saw those photos of how abused Chase was—it would turn things around quickly. All those emails she'd sent to the reporters had to break things open. Her job in the meantime was just to keep Chase and herself free. She drove along a lengthy schoolyard, kids playing soccer with garbage cans doubling as goalposts. Soon she'd be at Camp Lake Choctaw. She texted: *Tara wher r u?*

She got a text back. *At camp. Wher u been? U didn't answer calls, texts. Annie whole frickin world is after u.*

Okay, Annie thought with a nod. She turned to Chase. “Well, what do you think, little man? The whole frickin world is after us.”

At Camp Lake Choctaw she texted Tara to join her in the Chevy, and it didn’t take long for Tara to come running out and hop into the back seat. “Oh my God! Look at you!” Tara leaned over the seat and touched Annie’s hair. “And your eyes. You don’t even look like you.” Then she leaned way over, practically crawling into the front, to look at Chase. “Oh my God! You’ve really got him! Houston Monroe’s baby!”

Annie drove off, suddenly thinking that coming to talk to Tara maybe hadn’t been the best idea she’d ever had. Even so, it was good to be with her friend. Tara was always so positive and 24/7 excited about life.

Tara leaned over again and gave Annie a hug. “You’re famous, Annie. All the news shows, the online mags, the blogs are talking about you. You’re trending everywhere. You’re also…” she said but her words fell off, swallowed by the throb of the Chevy’s engine.

“What? What were you going to say?”

Tara shook her head.

Annie could sense her friend’s deep emotion. “Tara, please just say it. At this point it’ll be worse if you don’t.”

“Well.”

“Say it.”

Tara nodded. “There’s a rumor going around.”

“Go ahead.”

Tara frowned. “It’s that the ten million isn’t just for turning you in.”

“And?”

"It's for you…dead or alive."

They rode along in silence, the sun finally ducking below the horizon, darkness falling fast. Oh well, Annie thought. Dead or alive was no idle threat in Arizona where so many people legally carried guns. But now at least she figured things couldn't get any worse. And the truth, she reminded herself. They still had the truth on their side.

Finally Tara broke the quiet. "So anyway, why'd you kidnap him?"

"Oh, Tara, I didn't *kidnap* him. I rescued him from being abused."

"But, you just took him, just like that?"

"No, not *just like that*." She sighed. "It's complicated."

Tara put her hands on the seatback. "The cops interviewed me and all your friends and teachers, looking for clues. The only one who wouldn't talk to them was Stu."

Annie smiled. It felt like Stu was a real ally, and she needed all the allies she could get. Which reminded her of something. "Tara, let me use your phone, will you?"

"Why don't you use yours?"

"Come on, just let me use it."

Tara handed it over. "Who you calling?"

"My father."

Tara bit her lower lip. "Good luck with that." She leaned over and looked at Chase again. "Houston Monroe's baby! I can hardly believe it!"

"Daddy, it's Annie." She wedged the phone into her shoulder and drove with both hands.

"Annie, where are you? Are you okay? Is the baby okay?"

"I'm fine. The baby's fine."

"Where are you? Just tell me and I'll come get you."

She shook her head. "Sorry but I can't do that."

"Annie, now listen to me. I've hired a lawyer—I'm sure you realize that there are major consequences to what you've done."

"I'm doing the right thing."

"Annie, *listen to me*. The lawyer said it makes all the difference in the world what you do *right now*. Honey, I love you. I'm not going to lie to you. He said the only chance for leniency in your case is if you turn Chase over to the authorities *right now*."

"My case? Daddy, I've done nothing wrong." Annie glanced back at Tara for support. "Nothing. I'm saving this baby's life!"

Chase started crying.

"Is that the baby?" her father asked.

"Oh, I gotta go." Annie turned to say something to Tara, the phone slipping from her shoulder.

"Annie, look out!"

Annie stomped the brakes and the Chevy skidded till it smacked into the back of a mini-van.

"Oh no. Oh God no," Annie said under her breath. "I'll be nailed if they see my name on my driver's license." She swallowed hard as an older man, maybe forty, emerged from the mini-van and looked at his bumper. "Tara, give me your license."

"What!"

"Just give it to me!"

Tara nabbed her license from her purse and handed it over.

Annie climbed from the Chevy just as the driver of the mini-van got to her. He was a slight man, intelligent eyes, but his cheeks were full-blown red.

"What the hell were you doing?" the man said, shaking his

head. “Couldn’t you see me stopped there! Are you blind!” He looked at his bumper. It hung down a couple of inches but was still firmly attached. Cars were creeping around them.

“There doesn’t seem to be much damage,” Annie said.

“Not much damage?” The man scowled. “You know how much they’re going to charge me to fix this? Over a grand, easy.” He looked at Tara in the Chevy. “What, out for a little joy ride? Smoking marijuana with your friend?”

“Please, Mister. We weren’t joy riding. I’ve got a sick baby in the car seat. I was rushing him to the hospital and he was crying and so I reached down to comfort him and when I looked up it was too late.”

The man frowned and searched her eyes. Then he looked over her shoulder, the anger lines in his face softening. “You gotta sick kid?”

“A baby.”

He stepped toward the Chevy. He peeked through the windshield and down at Chase. He said, quieter and calmer now, “Just show me your license and give me your phone number. We can work this all out later.”

“Thank you so much, sir.” She handed him Tara’s license and ducked back into the Chevy. “Tara, you have a pen?”

“Blue or black ink?”

“Tara!”

Tara handed her a pen.

Annie turned back to the man.

“Doesn’t look much like you,” he said, holding the license up to her face.

Annie smiled. “I had a complete makeover.”

# Chapter Ten

Annie climbed back into the Chevy. "That was close." She gave Tara her license back and checked on Chase. She waited for the mini-van to pull off.

"Yeah, great, now you've got me involved in this too," Tara said but not meanly.

"You know I wouldn't have done it if the situation hadn't been so desperate." She nodded toward Chase and started the car. "Besides, I gave him *my* phone number."

"So really you're like a criminal now." Tara slipped her license into her purse. "I mean, like a good criminal like Robin Hood or something like that."

Annie rolled her eyes. "Yeah, something like that."

"Annie Hood."

"Tara, let me have your phone again."

Tara gave it to her.

Annie checked her email to see if any of the reporters had responded. Not a single one! They were all probably afraid of Monroe, but no matter, she wasn't going to let that stop her. She'd find a way to save Chase. It was just looking like it might take a little longer. She gave the phone back and when the mini-van left she drove off. "Tara, Chase and I are going to need a place to stay tonight."

"You mean to hide out."

"Well, yeah, but lose the criminal lingo already, will you? I'm doing something good. The only problem is nobody else understands that."

Tara nodded. "I don't know, Annie. You can stay at my

house, but I'm sure there might be cops watching it, since we're best friends."

"Yeah." Annie thought and thought about it. It wasn't that late, and with the net closing in on her and Chase maybe there was something she could still do tonight.

"You don't think you should turn him in?"

"Oh God. Are you telling me that even you don't believe me?"

Tara shrugged. "Oh, I believe you. But there's just so much stuff in the media about it. Everybody's outraged. It's hard not to be influenced by it."

"Do they ever mention a guy named Thaddeus?" She had to think to remember his last name. "Kostopoulos."

"Kost-octupus?"

"Tara."

"Okay, no. No, they don't talk about a Kost-anybody."

Annie sighed. She was cruising side streets. Trying to think.

"There is one guy they keep showing though."

"Who?"

"They didn't give a name. They just called him an accomplice. But you wouldn't be able to miss this guy. He has a big afro-like head of curly black hair. I mean, he's white, but his hair is really curly. And he's young and pretty hot too."

"What do they say about him?"

"Just that he's one of the kidnappers and if anyone has information about him to call the police."

"Okay." At least it sounded like Thad was still free.

"Gum?" Tara held out a stick.

Annie shook her head.

"Hey, think you could drop me at Target?" She slid the gum

into her mouth and crumpled the wrapper.

"Aren't your parents expecting you home?"

"Ah, not necessarily. I feed them all this Dr. Phil crap about parents needing to trust their teenagers and they buy it." She laughed.

Annie hated to lose Tara's company but what could she do? "Yeah, okay, but not a word of this to anyone."

"Uh, I kinda figured that much. But there is one thing I gotta tell you."

"What?" Annie's jaw tensed. "Tara, come on, quit prefacing all this stuff already."

Annie's friend took a deep breath. "Some of the jocks at Alameda—you know, the jerk ones led by chief jerk Henry Buck—are hunting you down. They're obsessed with getting the ten million dollar reward. They've been pressuring me to tell them where you are."

"All right. Fine. Thanks for the heads-up, but that's the least of my concerns at this point." They rolled into Target's parking lot. "And so who's all going to be there now?"

"God, I don't know. The Miller twins. Maybe Stu. Emily Johnson."

"Stu, really, you think he'll be there?"

"Yes'm." Tara laughed, mimicking Stu's Texas drawl. "I just love the way he talks."

Annie was thinking. "You have his cell number?"

"Yeah, why? You like him?"

"Not like that, but I think maybe he could help me and Chase."

Tara hesitated. "What if he's after the ten million too?"

Annie swallowed. "That's a chance I'll have to take."

Tara took out her pen, unfurled the gum wrapper and wrote his number.

"Thanks. And let me borrow your phone one more time."

* * *

"Sorry about having to sit in back, Stu." Annie'd called him and asked if he would come out to talk. They were driving in the Chevy toward the desert.

"Not a problem."

Annie marveled at how deep Stu's voice was, and Tara was right—he talked *so* slowly and with that big Texas drawl.

"Stu, listen. I'm going to cut to the chase. I know you hardly know me but I was hoping to ask a favor."

"All right."

"Well, you've heard about what's going on with me?"

"Yes'm."

"And you don't think badly of me?"

"I don't think bad of nobody till they give me a reason to. And you ain't given me no reason."

Annie eased out a sigh. She glanced at Stu in the rear view mirror. "Thank you for that, Stu. I wish more people were like you."

Annie told him the whole story about Monroe abusing Chase. When she finished she waited. Finally Stu spoke.

"All I can say is, from what you told me, I'd be fixin' to give Monroe a trimmin'."

"I'd like to too—not that I could—but the thing is, Stu, if you were to beat up Monroe that wouldn't help Chase any."

"What were you thinking of doing?"

"Tara told me you're good with computers."

"Yes'm."

"Well, maybe you could help me get the word out about Chase being abused." She caught his eye in the rear view mirror. "But I have to tell you, Stu, what I'm thinking of doing might be dangerous, very dangerous."

He nodded.

"I'll understand completely if you don't want to do it."

Stu rubbed his chin. "No. You've told me straight out what's what. I like that. And I wanna help that little baby too. So count me in."

* * *

Annie set a meet with Stu—she told him to bring Tara—at nine p.m. in the beer garden of La Contina restaurant on the outskirts of town. La Contina's beer garden was relatively dark and never crowded. Annie had a half hour to kill before the meet time so she stopped and bought another cheapie cell phone and called her father again.

He answered.

"Dad, it's Annie."

"Tell me where to meet you, honey."

Her shoulders slumped. "Dad, I'm going to see this through."

"Annie, are you *deliberately* disobeying me?"

She took a deep breath. "I see it as obeying my conscience."

Silence.

Annie said, "Are you there?"

"Honey, you're wrong about Monroe."

She bit her lip. "And how would you know that?"

"I know because I've been researching him non-stop since you took Chase."

She shrugged. "Dad, I'm going to do what I have to do. I'd really like to have your support but if you can't give it I understand." She turned onto Arrowhead Boulevard which would take her all the way to La Contina. A police cruiser was a half a block in front of her—she made a quick turn onto a side street. "Listen, I need to get going here."

Another stretch of silence.

"Goodbye, Dad."

"Annie, I met with Monroe."

"What?!"

"Honey, he's a decent and honorable man."

"Oh my God. What happened—you weren't so keen on him when you forbade me to work there."

She heard him take a deep breath. "Well, I've changed my mind about him."

"Why?"

"Honey, he came here to talk to me. We spoke over an hour. Like any parent, he just wants his child back."

"But I told you how he abused Chase."

"He told me you were concerned about that and said it was just a self-soothing technique he was employing, letting the baby cry itself to sleep so it wouldn't become overly dependent."

"He *abused* it, Dad."

"Honey, I insisted, over your mother's objections, to do the exact same thing with you when you were a baby."

Annie laughed scornfully. So Chase and her had something deep in common. And she was not going to let Chase suffer any more. "I gotta go, Dad. I'll call you later."

"Annie!"

She hit the end button.

*  *  *

La Contina's beer garden was like being in Acapulco. Twinkling white lights strung across open-air rafters. The floor blue brick. The restaurant wall was red and had a big blackboard with drink specials chalked in. A wooden fence, draped with Dos Equis banners, surrounded the rest of the beer garden. The sun long down, the air cooling. Friendly accordion music on the sound system. It smelled of spicy barbecue.

Annie had Chase in a front baby sling snug against her body. He was changed and fed and seemed to be enjoying the close connection with her as much as she was with him. She scanned the beer garden for Stu and Tara. They were in a far corner, sitting at a wrought iron table. Perfect.

"Thank you so much for coming, both of you."

Stu jumped up and pulled out a chair for her.

"Oh, thanks, Stu."

He nodded.

Tara said, "So how's it going, *Mom?*"

Annie smiled. She was starting to feel like a mom. It was an unusual feeling for sure but a good feeling too. "All right. It's going all right."

"I can't get over you as a redhead," Tara said. "Are you going to keep it red when this is all over?"

"Oh, I don't know, Tara. I guess I could always see if I like it. Honestly, I haven't had time to think about it." She adjusted Chase's pacifier. Annie figured she had a few minutes for small talk, and it felt so good to be with friends. "So, Stu, tell me, how do you like the valley so far?"

Stu straightened his shoulders. "Well, I like it just fine."

Annie was growing to love his accent—and he'd practically sung *fine*. "That's good." She turned to Tara. "And you, Miss Camp Lake Choctaw, how are the kiddies treating you?"

"Oh, they're a thrill a minute, let me tell you. A kid put his foot into a shoe with a scorpion in it today. His foot blew up like a balloon and I had to rush him to the hospital." Tara got up and walked over to Annie and Chase, her voice shifting into baby talk mode. "And how is this little guy?" She made a face at Chase and he smiled. "Yes, you're a real cutie, aren't you?"

A waitress came by and Annie ordered a coke. She munched on a taco chip from a big basket on the table. Yes, after living in non-stop drama it felt so good to relax with friends, but she didn't want to risk being out in public any longer than she had to. "Listen, you guys, I've come up with a plan to help Chase. I was hoping to run it by you. Actually, I was hoping you might help me."

Tara nodded.

Stu said, "Shoot."

Annie inhaled deeply. "I need to get the truth out about Monroe abusing Chase. That's the only way of saving him, so I figured I'd use my Facebook and Twitter accounts to do that, but ever since this thing with Monroe started, both of those accounts got hacked. Then I sent the photos to TV and newspaper reporters, but that didn't work. In fact, it's like nothing I've tried has worked. But I know Monroe is into computers big-time—I saw the computer room at his mansion and it's incredible—and when I heard Stu was into computers too a light bulb went off in my head."

"What about me?" Tara said, sipping her drink. "No light bulbs? And I've got *way* more friends and followers on Facebook and Twitter than you."

"I'm getting to you, Tara," Annie said. "Just hang with me a bit. Oh no."

Dr. Hakim walked—he was limping—into the beer garden with two Arabic-looking men. All three wore fine linen suits and shiny loafers with tassels. They were checking the drink specials on the blackboard.

"What, Annie?" Tara leaned toward her.

"Don't look," Annie said, lowering her head, "but that guy with the ponytail checking the blackboard over there works for Monroe."

"Wow," Tara said. "He's a hottie. What's his name?"

"Tara, I'm serious. Stop gawking."

Dr. Hakim and the other two men headed back into restaurant.

"All right," Annie said quickly. "What I was thinking is if Stu could somehow hack into Monroe's computers and get all Green Magic Waste Removal's customer email addresses, then we could send out an email blast to them with the photos I took of Chase at Monroe's."

No one said anything and Annie was feeling like maybe she'd just suggested the dumbest thing ever. "Green Magic has over three *million* customers in the valley."

Finally, Stu spoke. "We'd need to use an ESP."

Annie shrugged. She didn't know what that meant.

"But wouldn't that be considered spamming and isn't spamming illegal?" Tara said.

"Oh, Tara, I don't care about that. All I care about is saving Chase." Annie turned to Stu. "Do you think you could do it?"

"Mmm. I'm sure Monroe's got some pretty heavy cyber security. To a business like his, big data is everything and they protect it like gold."

"But you can do it?" Annie asked again, and just as she did,

Dr. Hakim and his friends walked back in and sat at the table next to theirs. Annie instinctively covered Chase's face. She caught Tara's eye and shook her head in warning.

"Yeah, yeah, I got it," Tara said.

Dr. Hakim glanced over and he and Annie caught eyes. Oh God, Annie thought. If Mrs. Kendall told the police about her new look he might recognize her. She turned back to Stu and speaking softly asked yet again, "So you can do it?"

Stu seemed to think about it. Finally he said, "One way or another, I reckon." He nodded his head firmly.

# Chapter Eleven

The next morning Annie woke up, Chase sleeping peacefully at her side, in yet another out of the way motel, this one to the east of the valley. She thought of all that had gone down last night. At the beer garden, Dr. Hakim had looked over several times. Annie ignored him. If Dr. Hakim had wanted to make trouble she knew Stu would defend them. Like they say, 'There are only two kinds of people in the world: the people that run to a fire, and the people that run from it.' Stu was the kind of person who ran to the fire.

Try as he might though Stu couldn't hack Monroe's computers. He told Annie they had *air gap encryption*, whatever that was. Annie couldn't follow all the details. She had a Plan B though. That plan was birthed when Stu said that although he couldn't obtain Green Magic's email addresses remotely, he had become familiar enough with Monroe's computers—he called it *computer architecture*—that if he could get into Monroe's computer room itself, he was sure he could.

Annie knowing that she could be caught any moment, and if she was, that her hopes of saving Chase were over, moved into action. She told Stu and Tara about the new plan. They were both game. She had Tara watch Chase. She bought a rope and some wrenches, and with the help of an eight-year-old kid's Youtube video made a grappling hook for Stu. She gave Stu the security code to Monroe's alarm system and drew up a floor plan for when he got over the perimeter wall, drawing him a path through the labyrinth of Monroe's mansion to get to the computer room. She gassed up the Chevy. She would be the bait in the plan, drawing everyone out of the mansion so Stu could enter unimpeded. Lastly they all synchronized their watches and set up a place to rendezvous afterward.

Annie knew well enough that if this plan failed, all hope of saving Chase would be lost, but she was determined the plan wasn't going to fail.

She would drive Stu—he leaving his car at the base of the mountain—out to Monroe's compound in the souped-up Chevy. Stu would go over the compound's perimeter wall and then once he had Green Magic's email addresses, he would hike down the mountain. Annie had warned him about rattlesnakes but Stu said he wasn't worried—they had plenty of rattlesnakes in Texas too. Annie asked if maybe he should have a gun. He'd shaken his head confidently. Annie was surprised he only had a couple of flash drives the size of cigarette lighters to put the three million email addresses on, but he explained that flash drives although small had huge capacities nowadays and chances were he wouldn't use half of one. He'd tested the grappling hook and was sure it would hold him. He had a canteen. Annie was amazed at how calm he was, speaking in his slow, steady Texas drawl.

She dropped him off a half a mile from the compound, thanking him, wishing him luck, thanking him again. She watched him in his camouflage clothing disappear into the mountain's scruffy bushes and cacti. God, she could hardly believe they were doing this. She put her phone on the seat next to her. She was to give Stu twenty minutes to get to the wall. Then she was to drive to the gate, and when Monroe and his lackeys came after her, call Stu.

It was the longest twenty minutes of her life. She dreaded to think of the risk Stu was taking. Had she been right to ask it of him? She thought of calling it off. She could come up with another plan, a better plan maybe. Yeah, she could come up with a better plan. She grabbed her phone, but as she began to punch in Stu's number, all she could see in her mind's eye was Chase's tear-stained face, his withering little body when he'd been at Monroe's.

She threw the phone onto the seat—the twenty minutes were up—and put the Chevy in gear. She drove to the compound's security gate and called Stu. "Just stay on the line, Stu," she said, rolling down her window. She looked into the main surveillance camera. "Monroe, it's Annie Rebarchek. I wanted to give you one last chance to come clean about Chase. If you do, confessing to the media all the abusive things you've done to him, I will deliver him to Sheriff Delgado." She barely got out the last word when a Jeep barreled down the drive.

She shut her window and blurted into her phone, "Okay, Stu!" She threw the Chevy into reverse and slammed her foot on the gas, smoke pouring over the windshield as she backed. She switched gears and peeled rubber flooring the car away from the compound. She'd planned her escape route, every single twist and turn on the steep mountain road. She felt she could get away, but even if she didn't she had high hopes Stu could pull off his end and get the email blast out to Green Magic's three million customers.

The Chevy powered along but Annie carried too much speed into a turn and the car fishtailed onto the gravel shoulder, dust and pebbles kicking high in the air behind. Annie glanced over the cliff. My God, she thought. She'd been inches from going over a two thousand foot drop. She was dizzy from vertigo but she was doing it—handling the turns and staying ahead of the Jeep. Then it was as if a rock pinged off the Chevy's hood. What the hell!

She looked up the mountain and saw Monroe standing there in a white suit on the edge of the road with a scoped rifle. A little puff of smoke issued from the rifle's barrel and the Chevy's back window shattered, glass shards spitting into the car, Annie feeling sharp pricks in her shoulders and the back of her neck. Damn it! Was he going to kill her?

She checked her rear view mirror and the Jeep was gaining on her. A bullet hit the rear driver's side window, more glass shards bursting across the interior. Annie vowed if she got out of this alive she was going to make Monroe pay. The Jeep was right on her tail. It was weird driving now, the glass shards all over and the roar of outside air ripping through the shattered windows. "Come on," Annie said to the Chevy. "You can do this."

She felt a jolt. The Jeep had slammed into the back of the Chevy. She checked her rear view mirror. It was Dr. Hakim. And he had a pistol. He was trying to steady his aim as he leaned out the driver's side window.

"Oh, no you don't." Annie hit the brakes, and the Jeep banged solidly into her again, Dr. Hakim's pistol clattering to the pavement.

"Yeah!" Annie yelled. "There you go!" Dr. Hakim's Jeep fell back and that gave Annie just enough time to wonder how Stu was faring. God, she hoped he was safe. She thought of Chase with Tara. She hoped Tara hadn't done anything foolish. And she really missed not having Chase with her. She felt a mother's bond with him. A mother's desire to protect him.

The Jeep pulled alongside her on the left, Annie's Chevy canyon-side. Dr. Hakim motioned for her to pull over.

"Not a chance!" Annie yelled.

A jolt as Dr. Hakim's Jeep slammed into the side of the

Chevy. "Oh my God!" The Chevy was thrust onto the guardrail-less shoulder again. Another flash of vertigo shot through Annie when she looked over the edge, but she managed to get the Chevy back up onto the pavement. The two vehicles raced to a sharp turn in the switchback. Annie floored the Chevy. Dr. Hakim kept pace alongside. Both of them wouldn't be able to handle the hairpin turn at that speed.

"Give it up, Hakim!" Annie yelled. The cars hurtled side by side, doors chafing, sparks flying. A deadly game of 'chicken.' Whoever panicked first would be dead.

Dr. Hakim yelled something but with the engines screaming and wind ripping through the Chevy Annie couldn't make it out. The cliff loomed. Dr. Hakim swerved into her and Annie pulled her hands across the wheel as if she were swerving back but didn't and instead jammed both feet on the brakes.

The Chevy spun and spun and spun—Annie waiting for the sensation of falling—to a halt inches from the cliff's edge. Annie looked around for Dr. Hakim but there was nothing. Then the sound of an explosion.

* * *

Now what? Annie thought as she backed from the cliff's edge and then continued down the mountain. She knew she had to ditch the Chevy fast and so pulled into a sand-filled runaway truck ramp. She could hear sirens so there was no time to waste. She had a screwdriver from making the grappling hook for Stu, so she was able to remove the New Mexico plate from the Chevy. But how was she going to walk around with a license plate? Anyway, she'd figure that out later, because now she had to move. The sirens were homing in. All kinds of sirens. Whining, blaring, screaming sirens. It was like the end of the world.

She couldn't walk on the road so she headed into the mountain. She'd gone hiking with her dad around Canyon Lake and he'd taught her how to watch for rattlesnakes, but even if she avoided the rattlers she couldn't avoid the danger of the heat. It had to be over a hundred and ten, and the mountain offered only the scantest shade. She'd need water very soon. She found a trail and walked half a mile until it hit her—she'd just been involved in the death of another human being. She felt a sinking, sick feeling in her gut.

She sat on a boulder, thoughts and emotions whirling. She'd had to do what she'd done. Monroe was shooting at her. Dr. Hakim was trying to push her off the cliff. And really she was just fighting for little Chase. Little Chase who couldn't fight for himself. No, she'd had to do what she'd done.

She stood. She hadn't even been thinking about rattlers—she wasn't going to be any good to Chase if she got bit and died on the mountain. And she was already parched. Just a few water-less hours in that kind of heat could be deadly. The trail was steep where she was walking and she had to lean back to counterbalance her forward momentum. Down in the valley, ghastly smoke rose. Dr. Hakim's Jeep. A funeral pyre, and ironically, the smoke added to the valley's 'brown cloud' Monroe was so determined to get rid of.

She neared the bottom. The sun screaming-hot. The back of her neck burning. Her mouth felt like it was full of sawdust. She wondered if Stu had gotten the three million email addresses, if he was all right. She wondered how Chase was. She was sure Tara was taking good care of him but even so, a host of things could have gone wrong. They were all to meet at three p.m. in the corner of an abandoned shopping mall near Superstition

Mountain, way on the other side of the valley. Annie was determined to make it there on time, but to do so she was going to need a car.

First she needed water. She stuffed the license plate into the back of her blouse and walked down side streets until she got to a convenience store. She grabbed a handful of candy bars and a two-liter bottle of water from the cooler. While she waited in line a news bulletin came on the ceiling-mounted TV. A talking-head newsperson. "A breaking story. Today at the west valley palatial estate of billionaire Houston Monroe there has been a wild scene of car chases and shootings. Police are still piecing together the details, and our Traci McDowell is on the scene with a live report. Traci, what can you tell us?"

The camera cut to a brash blonde holding a microphone. "Well, as you said, Don, police are still piecing together what happened, but we do know that at least two men are dead, one an associate of Houston Monroe's who was killed in a car chase by baby Chase's kidnapper."

Annie was next in line. She had to get out of there fast.

The reporter kept talking, while the screen flashed to a photo of Monroe holding a rifle. "Houston Monroe gallantly tried to save his associate and police are commending his courage."

Walking out of the store Annie heard: "And, Don, KVAL has obtained this exclusive video footage taken by Monroe's surveillance camera of the woman believed to be baby Chase's kidnapper." Annie turned to look. The video was of her in the Chevy, but she was in the shade and the video was blurry. She was gesturing with her hand. Even so, the video showed her with the short red hair and black contacts.

She hurried out of the store and crossed the street. What a

nightmare, she thought. She stood in a bus shelter, cars zipping past. She rinsed her hands with the water she'd bought, turned away from the street and removed the contacts. Then she took a long swig of the water and wolfed down a candy bar. The water and sugar flooded energy into her body and hope into her spirit. She could feel herself coming back to life. She noticed that not a few of the people going into the convenience store left their cars running. She checked her watch. 2:07. She had fifty-three minutes to get to the rendezvous with Stu and Tara.

She told herself everything she was doing was only to save Chase. If that meant stealing a car, that's what it meant. She'd return the car when all this craziness was over.

A woman with a white fluffy-haired poodle in her arms emerged from her car and went into the store. Annie crossed the street. Head down, glancing left and right, she made her way across the parking lot. Exhaust flowed from the car's muffler. Annie looked into the store. The woman and her dog were in the back by the coolers, and they were being occupied by a couple of kids petting the dog.

Annie walked directly to the woman's car and climbed in.

* * *

Annie drove the woman's car to a deserted field, removed the car's license plate and replaced it with the New Mexico one. It was as if she was running on auto-pilot—the depth of the emotional things she'd been experiencing short circuiting her ability to think—and something outside herself was directing her. Which maybe wasn't all bad because if she'd been forced to think of everything she was doing, she would've been overwhelmed. The way it was, she just saw herself as on a mission to save Chase. Everything revolved around that.

Her body continued to recover from dehydration as she drove, the water and sugar kicking in even more. The car was pleasant, some sort of Toyota, a big one, the air conditioning blowing refreshingly cool, a pretty, hooped dream-catcher, a golden feather dangling from it, hanging from the rear view mirror. The car smelled faintly of the poodle, and white fuzz on the passenger seat bore witness that it was the dog's reserved spot.

Finally, Annie's mind allowed her to think of some of the things that had just gone down. She had to let them in gradually. Monroe shooting at her. The glass shattering in the Chevy. And—she shook her head—Dr. Hakim going over the cliff. Her life had gone from looking like another ordinary summer working at Camp Lake Choctaw to a wild adventure. But it was more than an adventure. She felt like she was growing up too. Caring for Chase was making her feel what it was like to be a parent, what it was like to care about someone else's life more than her own.

Memories of the day continued to filter in as she drove, and she was thinking about what was coming up too. Maybe she should dye her hair black or maybe go punk and get a mohawk, because now everyone in the valley was going to be looking for a redhead with short hair from that news report. It all just seemed surreal. Something about the news report was nagging at her, too, a thought that wouldn't quite come to consciousness, as she pulled into the abandoned shopping mall for the rendezvous with Tara and Stu, Superstition Mountain towering nearby. She checked her watch. She was three minutes late. Tara's car was in the corner. Now what was that thought nagging her? She scanned the parking lot—no sign of Stu yet. Yeah, it had been something in the news report she'd heard at the convenience store. She'd been too wired to fully take in everything that had been said.

Tara climbed from her car. Her face was streaked with tears, her eyes bloodshot. Oh no, Annie thought, something happened to Chase. But that unconscious nagging thought from the news report was rising to the surface. Annie pulled up to her friend. The report had said *two* men were dead. Annie rolled down her window. “Tara, what’s wrong?”

Tara sniveled. “Oh God, you didn’t hear?”

Annie’s heart felt like it flew from her chest. “Is it Chase?”

Tara looked down, tears spilling from her eyes. “Oh God, Annie, Stu is dead.”

# Chapter Twelve

No, Annie thought. It can't be. She'd just been with Stu before she drove to Monroe's security gate. He just must be delayed in meeting them, that was all. Stu was too strong, too smart to have gotten killed. No, he'd be along. Tara was mistaken. And he'd probably gotten the three million email addresses too. No, Tara was definitely mistaken.

Reality intruded. Tara showed Annie her phone, the breaking news about Stu's death. The media was saying he was a thief, intent on stealing Monroe's priceless art collection. They were saying in a shootout he was gunned down by Monroe. Annie blew out a long breath. She could no longer deny that Stu was dead. She climbed from the Toyota and hugged her friend. "Oh my God, Tara."

"I can't believe it."

"And those news reports are lying. A shootout. Stu didn't even have a gun."

Tara sighed.

"Is Chase okay?"

"Yeah. He seemed sad when you left but yeah, he's fine. Come on." She led Annie to her car. Chase was in the back in a car seat.

Annie wiped the tears from her face, not wanting Chase to absorb her sadness. "Hello, little man." She took him in her arms, and again he glommed on to her as if she were life itself. She looked at Tara, who was trembling.

"Annie, I'm scared. If they killed Stu…"

"We'll be okay, Tara."

"Annie, I know you swore me to secrecy but I really need to talk to my parents and ask them what to do."

Annie nodded.

"I mean, what if they come to kill *us?*"

Annie shook her head. "They're not going to kill us. They're not going to kill us because we have the truth on our side."

"But that hasn't made any difference at all."

Annie gritted her teeth. "That's because I have to find a way to get the truth out there."

"But you've tried and it hasn't worked. You wrote all those reporters and none of them have done a thing."

"That's because they're all afraid of Monroe."

"So then there's no way to do it."

"There's one reporter who isn't afraid of him."

"So why doesn't he expose him?"

Annie frowned. "Because I've got what he needs to do that."

Tara shrugged.

"I've got the photos on my phone showing how Monroe abused Chase, and I need to get them to that reporter before he can do anything. Thing is, I don't know where he is, but come on, maybe we can find him."

Tara shook her head. "Can't do it, Annie. I've got to get home. I'm sure my parents are already freaking out not knowing where I am."

Annie nodded. She hugged her friend. "I love you, Tara." She watched Tara return to her car but before Tara got in Annie called, "Tara, the car seat for Chase. And let me have your phone. It will really help me."

"Sure." Tara undid the car seat and walked back with it. "I've got another phone at home anyway."

"And can I have your sunglasses? And let me have your scarf too."

Tara unfurled the scarf from her neck and gave her the sunglasses perched on top of her head.

Dusk was falling, low clouds moving in from the east spreading fine gray rain against the backdrop of Superstition Mountain. Annie settled Chase into the car seat next to her in the Toyota. She looked at him. He was her strength, her courage. She put the scarf over her head, slipped on the sunglasses and headed for the *Superstition Mountain Independent* in Apache Junction.

She parked a ways from the office. She knew with the ten million dollar bounty on her head she would be a huge target, but she had to risk everything because if she was found before the truth got out about Monroe's abuse, it was all over for Chase.

Sheer-faced Superstition Mountain looked different in every season, at every time of day and in every type of weather. It could be a snow-capped wintry peak in February or a fiery volcano-like crag in July, but now, gray sheets of rain blending with a fog rolling in, it was a mysterious, smoky behemoth that loomed over tiny Apache Junction like an evil monster. Annie covered Chase up because of the rain, and it didn't hurt to hide his identity either, and started slowly, carefully, down the street.

With every step, the smell of rain pungent, the mist coating her face, Annie felt like the mountain was watching her, as if it were alive, or perhaps as if its spirits danced around her. Part of her knew that attempting to find Thad there was foolish. He wouldn't be in the *Superstition Mountain Independent's* office, as it certainly was being staked-out 24/7 by Sheriff Delgado's deputies in case he returned. Yet she felt compelled to take one more step, to turn one more corner, as if the misty mountain behind her was forcing her on.

Finally, the *Independent's* office came into view. The blinds were drawn but a light inside was discernible. In the newspaper box out front, Annie read the headline covering the entire front page of the *Superstition Mountain Independent*: $10 MILLION REWARD FOR KIDNAPPER.

"That's a lot of money, ten million," came a voice from over her shoulder.

Annie nodded, as if the voice had come from within her own mind. "It's crazy is what it is," she said. Then she realized what was happening and turned.

A Native American man, in his fifties but it was hard to say, powerful and broad shouldered, his graying hair parted in the middle, ponytails, darker, falling on the sides of his chest, stood motionless in a tan sleeveless hunting vest. His face was heavily creased and he stared straight ahead. "Wish I knew who the kidnapper was," he said. "I could sure use ten million, couldn't you?"

Annie laughed and looked back at the office. The man wasn't threatening. In fact, he was a friendly, peaceful presence. "Uh, sure."

"I think it's kind of funny, don't you, that it's raining and dark and you're wearing sunglasses."

She turned back to him.

"Annie," he added.

A shiver rattled through her. She removed the sunglasses. "Who…who are you?"

"I am Eli."

"What do you want?"

"I want only to serve the Great Spirit."

Somehow Eli's answer, cryptic as it was, didn't seem crazy and his presence remained calming. She turned to look at the newspaper office and the light within.

"Thad's not there," Eli said. "Come back tomorrow. Not here. Meet him at the high school at eight in the morning." He nodded. "The high school, there's only one, is just down the street. Usually no one's around in summertime."

Annie cradled Chase and thought of the implications of all Eli was saying. He could easily overpower her and he would be ten million dollars richer. "Why are you doing this?"

But when she turned to look he was gone.

* * *

Annie wasn't so sure it was a good idea to have borrowed Tara's phone. She read article after article about Stu's death, or sensationalistic articles about how evil she was. That or articles about how angelic Monroe was and what a hero he was to offer the ten million dollar reward. But the encounter with Eli had been a gift. She wished she'd had a chance to talk to him more. Now all she could do was speculate as to what his deal was. Thad must've told him to keep an eye out for her, but how he could've disappeared so quickly she'd never know.

One more fitful night in an out of the way motel and the morning came quickly, and with it the memory of Stu's death and a deep sadness, but she resolved to keep going for Chase's sake. She had to. She gave him a bath and fed him. Now it was just a question of waiting till eight to meet Thad at the high school. She tied her scarf tight on the top of her head, put on Tara's sunglasses and drove back to Apache Junction. The rain from the previous night had ended and it was a little cooler, only ninety. She turned into one of the high school's immense parking lots. She was sure

Thad would be able to find her—hers was the only car there.

She was so looking forward to seeing him. For how he could help Chase but, when she was honest with herself, just to see him too. He was smart, handsome, sincere and kind. Just the type of man she'd dreamed of. Only she had to dismiss those thoughts for now. Now it had to be all about saving Chase. She got out of the Toyota and collected him from the car seat. She didn't know how all this was supposed to go down. With Chase in her arms, she meandered to a broad athletic field with several baseball diamonds. She glanced at her phone. 8:07. Yes, Eli had said 8:00 a.m. but she trusted him. And she trusted Thad.

A little four-door yellow car entered the parking lot. Should she go to it? Absolutely nobody else was around. It had to be Thad, right? No, she told herself. All Eli had said was to show up. She'd showed up and now she would wait. But maybe she should wait closer to the Toyota. It was her lifeline. Out in the open with Chase she felt vulnerable. She was, after all, worth ten million dollars to anybody and everybody. The yellow car headed toward her. She squinted and looked hard and now she could see that there were several guys in the car—and that Thad wasn't one of them. She hurried her pace for the Toyota.

The yellow car swerved in front of her, its windows going down. Annie pulled Chase close to her breast. It looked like four high school jocks—more than likely football players—stuffed into the little car. The one in front with beefy sideburns and a thick neck asked, "Excuse me, do you know what field Prospector's football practice is supposed to be on?"

Annie shook her head. "Sorry." She walked on but the car rolled along with her.

"You have no idea?" said the side-burned one.

Another head shake.

One of the jocks in the back seat said, “Leave her alone, Stan. Come on, let’s go.”

The side-burned one pushed at the guy and said, “No, no.” He turned back to Annie. “Hey, you’re kind of young to be a mom, aren’t you?”

Annie kept walking but the car was angling her away from the Toyota. Her breathing quickened. Her heart pounding. She clutched Chase even tighter.

“Yeah, you could be that kidnapper on TV for all I know. Maybe we ought to make a citizen’s arrest and search you or something. Yeah, let’s see some I.D.” The car swerved in front of her, forcing her to stop.

A dark green Mustang, its accelerating engine throbbing, spun into the parking lot. It drew a beeline on the yellow car and Annie. Its tires smoked as it screeched to a halt. Thad jumped out. He was all in black, black pants, a tight black t-shirt, mirrored shades. He walked at the yellow car. “What’s going on here?” He bent low and looked inside. “What are you boys doing?”

“Who are you, slick?” said the side-burned one, perhaps emboldened by his size advantage and having three big friends with him.

Thad reached in and grabbed him by the throat. “I’m the one that told you to get the hell out of here.” He shoved him viciously back into the car. “Any more questions?”

The side-burned one, coughing, turned to the driver. “Let’s get the hell out of here! The guy’s a psycho!” The yellow car, its windows going up, peeled out of the lot.

Annie found herself smiling. “Well, that was good timing.”

“Are you okay?”

She nodded.

"And the baby?"

"Yeah." She shrugged. "Where'd you learn to be so bold?"

He didn't answer.

"Thad?"

"Afghanistan."

She took off her sunglasses and asked *what?* with her eyes.

"I was an aid worker and the Taliban didn't take kindly to aid workers. They thought…" He looked off. "…we were spreading diseases. I learned if you wanted to help the people there, you had to be tough."

"Okay." She stepped closer.

"So." He inhaled, scanning the area. "We shouldn't waste any time."

"No." She gazed at him. "I don't want to seem inappropriate here or anything, but…uh…I missed you." She swallowed.

He nodded. "Yeah. Likewise."

She smiled. "I've got this." She reached into her pocket and pulled out her phone. "It's got all the pics I took of Chase at Monroe's, and not a single reporter I sent them to responded, so I figure you might as well try your luck."

He took the phone with a nod. "I'll send them out right away and I'll have to because I've had a lot of heat on me lately. If you hadn't come by the office and Eli hadn't been there, I wouldn't have been able to find you. They've been all over me."

"They?"

Thad shook his head. "Sheriff Delgado's got his whole department on this case. He's a maniac. He hates the media but at the same time thrives on being in its spotlight, and he has promised publicly that he will crack this case in twenty-four hours. Him and his deputies are breaking all the rules to prove him right."

"But you're a step ahead of them?"

He frowned. "Not really. I can't compete with those kind of numbers, that much firepower. Then if you consider the lengths Monroe is going to and the ten million dollar reward, it just gets worse."

"So what do we do?"

"Well, I've got an in with the head of the Peace Corps, and I'm going to send him the photos, and he's promised to forward them to all fifty United States Senators. It's a can't miss, Annie. Even if the senators don't believe Monroe is guilty, they won't be able to deny getting the emails and photos, and they will have to publicly respond. Monroe's abuse will be forced into the public's awareness. The legal system will have to follow suit."

"Sounds good." Annie stepped even closer. She gazed up at him.

He put one arm around her shoulder, then the other, and he pulled her and Chase close. He leaned in to kiss…

Engines roaring, sirens blaring, five police cruisers and a black sedan charged down the road to the high school. Thad broke the hug. "Go. They don't have the intelligence that you're here, so they're after me. I'll keep them occupied as long as I can. When things settle down contact Eli again."

Annie wanted to say it. She whispered, "I love you."

He nodded. "Here take this." He pulled a revolver from the back of his pants.

"I don't want that."

"Just take it. Now go. Hurry."

She grabbed the gun and ran to the Toyota as the police cars and the black sedan barreled into the parking lot.

Annie hurriedly strapped Chase into the car seat and jumped in. Thad was already tearing out of the lot, a corridor of burning rubber smoke left behind him like a jet vapor trail. The Mustang accelerated tremendously around the back of the high school, the police cruisers and black sedan in hot pursuit. Just then a slew of police cars swirled around the opposite end of the building. Thad was cut off. He swung the Mustang in a one-eighty, the car's tires burning smoke like they were on fire, and wedged to a halt.

The Mustang didn't budge. The police cruisers and the black sedan screeched to halts. Uniformed deputies jumped out and crouched behind open car doors with shotguns leveled at the Mustang.

Slowly the Mustang's door opened, as simultaneously did the black sedan's, and with hands up, Thad emerged. He stood motionless, hands held high. Meanwhile a man, a hefty uniformed man wearing eyeglasses, that even though she was a ways off Annie recognized as Sheriff Delgado, climbed from the black sedan. Annie was nearly out of the parking lot but she slowed when Delgado pulled out a high-powered rifle with a scope on it and pointed it at Thad. Annie gripped the steering wheel so tightly, her eyes glued to the scene, as she drifted along. She gasped for a breath. But soon the high school building blocked her line of sight. "Oh," she cried. She glanced at Chase in the car seat. "Oh God," she said as she drove off.

* * *

Annie drove off listening and not listening for the sound of a gunshot. She had such a bad feeling about how Delgado had emerged from the black sedan and leveled the deadly rifle at Thad. Then feeling the need to stay positive she turned her thoughts to saving Chase. There'd been no point in staying in the parking lot to help Thad. All it would've done was given them Chase. Game over. And if Thad had been shot, it was better that she didn't know. At least now she could harbor the illusion that he was still alive.

She reminded herself that it was all about Chase. She looked at the pistol Thad had given her lying on the passenger seat. The gun was taking things to a whole new level. Then it hit her—the photos. She'd given Thad her phone with the photos incriminating Monroe. She almost turned back because the photos were the only way of getting word out of Monroe's abuse, but it was too late now.

But wait. Wait. She realized she didn't need to get the photos from her phone. She'd sent the emails with the photos as attachments to the TV and newspaper reporters. All she had to do was access her email and the photos would be there. She sighed a huge sigh of relief.

A host of police cruisers, lights flashing, sirens screaming, raced down the street toward her. She threw the pistol into the glove compartment, took a deep breath and thought, *well, if this is it, this is it*. But the cruisers ripped by, heading for the high school—and Thad.

She wiped the sweat from her forehead. If anybody could get out of that mess, it was Thad. His courage, his cool was inspiring. And she was glad she told him she loved him. At the time the words had just seemed to flow from her mouth of their own accord. She wondered if he loved her too. Ah, that was crazy, she told herself. They barely knew each other. But Thad was a man worthy of love. That much was sure. And he'd nodded when she'd told him she loved him. That could only be a good sign.

But Chase, Chase, Chase. Yes, it was all about Chase now. And she still had the photos. As soon as she felt she could she pulled to the side of the road to check her email on Tara's phone. She didn't get in to her email account. She must've used the wrong password. Figures, she thought. She was still shaky from the scene at the high school. She tried again. Same result. She checked her email address. It was right. Okay, she tried again, typing very slowly. Oh my God! She tried again. She couldn't get in.

It had to be Monroe. She shook her head. He must've blocked her account. He was cutting her off at every turn. Still, she tried to bolster herself, she had the truth on her side. Yes, she had the truth on her side. And…she opened the glove compartment and looked at the deadly pistol. She'd always been against violence of any kind but she remembered Monroe shooting at her on the mountain, and Sheriff Delgado leveling the high-powered rifle at Thad. No, she nodded and drew in a deep breath. She was glad she had the gun.

# Chapter Thirteen

First things first—Annie needed to make sure Chase was safe. So she headed back to Justiceburg. She knew going there was a risk, but the fact of the matter was that everything was a risk at this point. She drove to the Salamander Beauty Salon there—and she needed to remember that Chase was Frank to them—where she'd been treated so kindly, and discreetly, by the stylist Beatrice Parker. And she figured probably half the valley knew she had red hair by now. She wouldn't be able to change her hair color fast enough.

She walked in with baby Chase in the carry basket from the car seat. Beatrice Parker had a client in the chair, and a few women sat under hair dryers. Beatrice held the comb and scissors away from the woman's head and looked at Annie in the mirror. "You back for more already, girl?"

Annie wanted her hair dyed black, deciding to pass on the idea of getting a mohawk—not many mothers had mohawks, and anyway a mohawk would have drawn more attention than it would've avoided. "Up for a change of pace is all."

"Already? Oh my goodness." Beatrice laughed, her pretty gray eyes smiling. "Well, at the Salamander the customer is *always* right. I'll be with you as soon as I finish up here, hon."

Annie settled Chase in. Then she took out Tara's phone and thumbed through various news outlets. Nothing new about Thad. Which wasn't surprising. Sheriff Delgado had the reputation of withholding information from the media. And she couldn't help but wonder about the pistol Thad had given her. Why did he have it with him? And she wondered if he was about more than he'd told her. A whole lot more. He was just so knowledgeable and worldly, which sharp reporters often were, but how many of them had worked in Afghanistan and carried guns?

Beatrice was blow-drying the woman's hair. When she was done she held up a mirror at multiple angles. "Uh-huh?" she said. "Whatcha think?"

The woman left, and Annie, her thoughts swirling, was next. She climbed into the chair.

"So." Beatrice stood back and looked at Annie in the mirror. "What are you thinking, Andrea?"

Annie was surprised and more than a little touched Beatrice remembered her name, well, sort of her name anyway. "Uh, I'd say the color of your hair."

"Black?" Beatrice's eyes widened. "Really?"

Annie realized what a nut she must look like. From brown to red to black. She nodded.

"But not another cut?"

Another nod. "Maybe you could surprise me this time. Just so it flatters my face."

Beatrice laughed and pulled gently at Annie's hair. "Thing is it's getting a little short as it is, so it's going to be pretty short."

"Short is good. Brittany Spears shaved her head. It worked for her."

"Oh wow. Well." Beatrice fixed her eyes on Annie's in the mirror. "I am stopping short of that. Stylist's prerogative."

Annie exhaled. It felt good to have such a sympathetic, friendly person so close, and as Beatrice massaged the dye into her hair Annie found herself relaxing and chatting freely. Finally, as was expected, seeing how it was everywhere in the media, Beatrice brought up the kidnapping of Monroe's baby and the ten million dollar reward.

"Just think," she said. "How would you feel if you had a ten million dollar bounty out on *you?*"

Annie without thinking twice told the truth. "I'd be angry."

"Ha ha." Beatrice was all nods. "Me too, Andrea. Definitely." She looked at the women under the hair dryers, who were a ways off, bent toward Annie's ear and said softly, "And personally I wonder if there isn't more going on than what the TV people are telling us. I sometimes wonder about Mr. hoity-toity billionaire Monroe living in his compound up on the mountain like some kind of god on Mt. Olympus. It's not natural if you ask me."

Annie was pleasantly surprised by what Beatrice said. At least one person in the valley was suspicious of Monroe. After the dye was thoroughly massaged in, Annie joined Chase and the women sitting under the dryers to wait for the dye to set. Her mind, more relaxed than it had been in days, flowed easily. Thinking of all the things she'd tried to save Chase, they all seemed to involve one common thread—none of them had involved confronting Monroe directly.

Yes, she was mega-wary of Monroe. Yes, he'd shot at her. Yes, he'd killed Stu. But even with all that, Annie couldn't deny that whenever she'd spoken with him, he had conveyed an air of reasonableness. She didn't trust him, no, but she'd always been able to talk with him. Anyway, as things stood, contacting him was the best she could come up with and figured it was worth a try. And if worse came to worse she had the pistol.

She was half listening to Beatrice as she cut—and chattered on pleasantly—someone else's hair. As Annie continued to zone out, the ideas kept coming. They were coming fast. She took out Tara's phone and drafted an email to Monroe. She read it five times, tweaking it every go-through. She had it perfect but now it was time for the dye to be washed out of her hair.

Leaning back in the sink, the fragrant smell of the shampoo in the air, Annie relaxed even more as the warm water ran gently over her head and Beatrice softly massaged the shampoo into her hair and chattered on.

When Beatrice was done, Annie asked if there was any chance Beatrice could watch 'Frank' tomorrow.

* * *

Beatrice had agreed to watch the baby. Annie had driven around and sent a score of emails back and forth with Monroe to nail down the terms of their meeting. It was all set. Annie knew enough from her father about the art of the deal, and she knew Monroe didn't become a billionaire without being able to compromise and find a win-win solution to tricky problems. So this was a tricky problem, a very tricky problem, but solvable.

They were to meet at Terahawk Peak, one of the Dueling Peaks—the other being the adjacent Stony Peak—in the Superstition Mountain range, and part of their agreement was that Monroe arrive alone. In fact, he was to drive only to the last switchback in the mountain road leading to the peak and then walk the rest of the way. The understanding was that Chase would not be there, and if anything were to go wrong, a full news release as to their meeting would go public.

The meeting was to be at ten a.m. Annie dropped off Chase at the Salamander and headed out early. The sky clouded over as she drove down Highway 60, Superstition Mountain appearing like a hazy Sphinx in the distance. Annie'd meant to text her father on Tara's phone on the way there but had forgotten the phone at the motel room. She hoped it wasn't a bad omen.

She didn't forget the pistol.

By the time she got to the mountains a fine mist was collecting on the Toyota's windshield. Then the precipitation increased to the point where she needed to flip on her wipers. When she reached the last incline on the road to Terahawk Peak, the car's wheels were slipping in the muddy silt.

Annie was familiar with Terahawk Peak—which along with Stony Peak were the two highest points in the Superstition range —from when her father used to bring her there for picnics and paternal philosophizing. The place was the same as she remembered but with the rapidly changing weather, thunder growling in the distance, and dark clouds rolling over Superstition Mountain like a black carpet, it suddenly seemed dangerous as hell, spooky. Her heart pounded hard as she watched Monroe's white SUV wind up the switchback road. The SUV stopped a couple hundred yards off, like they'd agreed, and Monroe climbed out and started walking.

When he reached her, he stood panting, coughing into the sleeve of his white warm-up suit, which was spotted by raindrops blown by the freshening wind. He looked her in the eye with an expression that gave away little. "Well, here I am."

"Thank you for coming."

He nodded.

"Mr. Monroe, I'm going to tell you up front that all I want is for Chase to be safe and healthy."

"I want the very same."

See, she could at least talk to the man, she figured, even if he was lying through his teeth. "So it's just a question of meeting in the middle somewhere?"

In the distance, gauzy patches of gray rain were scattered

about the mountains, hanging slanted in the overcast sky like dirty shower curtains, but closer, the black clouds continued to pour over Superstition Mountain, turning the morning sky nearly evening-dark. A low crash of thunder bruised across the land, echoing.

When the thunder finally exhausted itself, Monroe said, “No, Annie, it’s a question of you breaking the law is what it is. Several laws, in fact.”

“As did you.”

“You killed Dr. Hakim.”

“You shot at me.”

Monroe shook his head and put his hand to his forehead.

Annie narrowed her eyes at him. “All right. Can we cut the ‘who did what’ blame game and come to an agreement that will benefit Chase?”

“There’s no agreement to come to.”

“Then why are you here, Mr. Monroe?”

“You know, Annie, in your emails you said you were reasonable, and that you valued my reasonableness. You think you know what’s best for Chase. I think I do. And yet you insist your way is the only way. Not very reasonable.”

“Because *you’re* not helping him!”

He scoffed, throwing his head back.

“You’re killing him!”

“Oh, for God’s sake. What are you talking about? I had Chase at Mayo Clinic for a physical just two weeks ago. His blood-work is optimal.”

“His blood-work may be, but with you his soul, his heart, his will to live was *dying*.”

Monroe laughed. “You know what, Annie, I told you before I

enjoyed a certain spunk in your personality, but there are two kinds of spunk. The spunk of people who are with you, and the spunk of those against you. The former are a dream, the latter a disaster. I was hoping you would see the light. I really could've used somebody like you on my team. You truly could have helped me—hell, you could've helped the world—in my work."

Annie knew he was referring to his eugenics experiments and she was dying to broach what his 'wife,' Vivian Sanchez, had told her about them, but she'd promised Vivian not to and would keep her word. "What you were doing to Chase wasn't right."

"And I say what you're doing isn't. In fact, not just what I say but what the whole valley says."

"Not the whole valley."

"No?" Monroe raised his hand, and the SUV's lights flashed on and it started up the last incline. "Here's someone in the valley who thinks that what you're doing isn't right."

"You swore you'd come alone!"

He waved the SUV to him. It pulled to a sudden halt and out climbed Annie's father.

What?! Annie's nostrils flared.

"Annie," her father called, walking up to her and Monroe. "This has gone on long enough. Now come with Mr. Monroe and me. Annie, Mr. Monroe has pledged to do everything in his power to help you if you come with us right now. Isn't that right, Houston?"

"What?! Dad, how could you do this?!"

"Annie, Annie," her father said, shaking his head. "In this particular instance, Houston is right. Honey, for God's sake, Chase is his son."

"He was killing him!"

"Honey." Her father walked at her. "You're hysterical—"

Annie kicked dirt at him. "Oh, if you think I'm hysterical now you just wait and see!"

"Annie, stop!" her father commanded. "Now you're coming with us. Get in the SUV."

Annie swallowed hard. It was the old subservience to male authority issue that had dominated her entire life. She took a step toward the SUV.

"That's my girl."

Monroe nodded.

She stopped. She took a deep breath and when she exhaled she felt like she was breathing out fire. "You can both go to hell!" She headed for the Toyota.

Her father and Monroe ran at her.

"No!" She spun around and whipped out Thad's pistol. "Back off! Both of you!"

"Annie!" Her father slowed but kept coming. "Now you give me that gun right now."

She leveled the revolver at his chest and shook her head slowly. "Stop walking, Dad." She squinted one eye down the barrel.

"My God, Annie, what's gotten into you?" her father said, but he stopped.

"Let her go, Tim," Monroe said and he put a hand on Annie's father's shoulder. "The whole base of the mountain is surrounded with Sheriff Delgado's men. She could never get away."

Annie kept the gun on the men as she walked backward, tripping a little over a rock, to the Toyota.

"Is that what you want, honey?" her father called. "To deal with all the Sheriff's deputies with their shotguns trained on you?"

Annie laughed. "Maybe you should ask Monroe about when he shot at me." Her jaw tensed. "And what do I want? I want to help a defenseless baby is what I want."

# Chapter Fourteen

Annie was running out of options. She'd thought meeting Monroe one on one might work. She'd had to take the chance. Maybe she should have known he would betray her, but that her father had become buddy-buddy with him was what really rocked her. Now, even with the news release Beatrice Parker would send, if she couldn't get back to Chase, Chase was sunk. She climbed into the Toyota. The black clouds pouring over Superstition Mountain had made their way to Terahawk Peak and weighty raindrops began to fall, splashing sporadically onto the Toyota's windshield. Annie flicked on the wipers and drove past Monroe's SUV. With Delgado's deputies waiting at the base of the mountain, she felt like she was driving to her doom, but she couldn't think of anything else to do. Lightning flashed overhead and thunder cracked, and it was as if the thunder really unleashed the rain.

Funny, Annie thought, this place gets hardly any rain all year, and now that this meeting—perhaps this evil meeting—has taken place, it's storming. She turned the wipers onto the high speed and carefully drove down the steep switchback road. Lightning flashed in front of her, illuminating the cacti, boulders and sagebrush on the mountainside. She would've normally stopped and waited for better visibility but she could make out the headlights of Monroe's SUV following behind. Ah, she thought, there were no good options. There'd be no way to elude Sheriff Delgado's men at the base of mountain. There was only one road in and out. More lightning flashed and a thunderclap rocked the Toyota. Maybe she'd die from a lightning strike. The irony that would be. She checked her rear view mirror again—Monroe was hanging right behind her. She shook her head. Her father. He must've been blinded by Monroe's success. That's all there was to it. But to lose his support hurt. It hurt a lot.

Again she checked the mirror. She wondered what would happen if she stopped? She remembered her mother's saying: 'Desperate situations call for drastic measures.' Yeah, if she was going to get out of this one, it was going to take something drastic. She gritted her teeth. She wasn't letting Chase down. That was all she knew. She had the pistol. She stopped. Monroe's SUV settled in behind her.

A tremendous branching lightning streak lit up the sky, the thunderclap simultaneous, and the rain gushed now, rainwater seeping steadily down the road. Maybe, Annie was thinking. Just maybe she could escape in the confusion of the storm on foot. Ah, but Monroe had said the entire perimeter of the mountain was surrounded. Drastic measures, she reminded herself. Drastic measures. Monroe's men couldn't be everywhere. She tucked the pistol tightly into her jean shorts and climbed from the Toyota. She kept her eyes on Monroe's SUV as she crossed the road, the driving rain lashing her eyes, and the cascading water running down the road soaking her shoes, splashing up onto her ankles. The driver's-side door of the SUV opened. She heard sharp, arguing shouts exchanged. It was too dark and rainy to see who got out, but as she descended into a gully running alongside the road, she thought she heard her father calling her name.

She started running. It was crazy running in the rain. It was so dark she could hardly see a thing and she would step on a rock and almost fall, or a foot would land in a depression and her ankle would jerk. But she wasn't giving in to Monroe. She hid behind a rock outcropping. Again she heard her name called or at least she thought she did, the downpour slapping the earth making it impossible to be sure. Lightning flashed, lighting up the rocks, boulders and sagebrush around her. Whoever was calling wasn't going to catch her, she resolved, and she continued blundering her way down.

Oh. She tripped and fell, her forearms crashing hard onto the rocks. She lay there in the rain, lightning criss-crossing the sky above, thunder reverberating, scraping the earth below. Monroe would get her now for sure. Her shorts and top were drenched, her forearms bruised. She struggled to her knees and looked behind her up the mountain. No one. That she could see in the blur of the deluge anyway. She stood.

She surveyed the situation. She could go down a steep ravine, the most direct route, but if she did, she'd have to go so very carefully, and slowly—and still might kill herself in the process. Or she could go down a moderately sloped gully. Lightning flashed, thunder chasing it. She felt like there was evil in the lightning somehow. Being so high in the mountain the lightning had such a short distance to travel. She felt like it was trying to kill her. She took a deep breath and shook off the scary thought. And anyway if the lightning didn't kill her, Sheriff Delgado's deputies probably would. Or maybe a rattlesnake. A million things could kill her, she figured, but *while she was alive* she would do everything in her power to get back to Chase.

She chose the gully. The downpour, thank God, was finally easing. She wiped her face and started down. Now the biggest danger was Sheriff Delgado and his trigger-happy deputies. They were as evil as the lightning.

There they were. The lights on their cruisers flashing. Ten, twenty cars flanking the only road, deputies in yellow slickers with shotguns, some with German Shepherds, standing there like a wall. She hid behind a massive boulder in the middle of the gully. She was thinking she could hike to the other side of the mountain, but that would take days, and there was no guarantee it wouldn't be as Monroe had said that the entire mountain was surrounded. She could wait them out. She shook her head. Surviving on an Arizona mountain without food or water in the summer was impossible. She could head back up the gully and make her way to the Toyota, but surely Monroe was all over it by now. She felt the pistol in the back of her waistband. Superstition Mountain had a gunfighter lore, the heart of the Wild West—she could shoot her way out.

Well, she wouldn't mind shooting a few people right now, but she laughed at the thought. No, there was nothing she could do. Nothing. She was stuck. Stuck. Monroe had won.

Then she saw the deputies pointing up at the mountain. What the hell. It was like they were pointing directly at her. But then they grabbed their dogs and ran for their cruisers. Annie shrugged. It was the strangest thing she'd ever seen. They jumped into their cruisers and were clearing out. They sped away. Leaving her free to walk down the gully and leave untouched. It was like…a miracle.

Then she heard it.

The sound of running water. She turned. Water was seeping down the gully, but not the dribble-like seeping that had been on the road—this was a little river! Flash flood!

Nowhere to go.

She looked to her left and right, nothing but sheer-faced cliffs on either side. The sound of the water got louder, rushing. She had just seconds before it hit. Her only protection was the boulder she'd been hiding behind. It was massive. She quickly circled behind it. Oh! The water hit her feet, splashing up to her knees. Seemingly placid from a distance, the rushing water pulled at her feet like invisible grabbing hands. The boulder was breaking most of the water's power, but as the volume of water increased, the rushing and churning water now roaring, it was clear she wouldn't be able to hold out there much longer.

Nowhere to go.

The raging water rushed by on both sides, wall to wall filling the gully. Only one chance. She found a handhold in the boulder, and then another. She gripped the boulder with all her might, the power of the water pulling against her strength. Trees, cacti, crushed by the weight of the charging water, whooshed past. She had to climb this boulder or she would share their fate. Lifting a foot up the boulder was like lifting a lead weight. It wasn't going to happen. Her strength was giving out.

In a way it would be a relief to let go. To quit this crazy inhuman effort. But then she thought of Chase, and of what his fate would be without her. She raised her foot and found a place for it in the boulder. She lifted the other foot and found a place for it. The pressure of the water fell off and, slowly, laboriously, she climbed to the top of the boulder. And now—oh God—she could see the full brunt of the wall of muddy, debris-strewn water rushing at her. The boulder, which had seemed so huge in the dry gully, now seemed a mere rock. And the flow of water was intensifying, rising, as if an ocean had been released somewhere up high in the mountain.

Annie sucked in air. Her exhausted body desperately needed to recover. A fallen pine tree, huge, cascaded down with the flood. It was headed straight at her. "No!" It crashed powerfully into the boulder, dislodging its solidity. Oh my God. Annie looked quickly down the mountainside. Trees, cacti, that stood in the onrushing water's path snapped like matchsticks. And—oh no—the boulder she sat on began to shift. She looked back up the mountain. Another boulder, as big as a pickup truck, was tumbling down with the torrent.

Nowhere to go.

The impact of the boulder hitting her boulder was like two mountains colliding. And her boulder was giving way now, turning, slowly, gradually, unmistakably, to join the onrushing water. She scrambled to stay atop it as it shifted. She scrambled to stay alive. She scrambled for Chase. Then the boulder gave way and...

Water.

Cold, very cold water. Taking her. Charging her. Plummeting her down the gully. No time to think. To react. Her body smashing into things. Gasping for breath. Rushing. Banging. Out of control. Flipped onto her back, caught a glimpse of sky, grabbed a breath, sucked right back under, tumbling, caught in the wall of rushing water, but a wall of water filled with trees and boulders and cacti. A wall of water, holding her down, stealing her breath, her life. She flashed to the surface. Another breath. Then right back down. Tumbling, bruising, dying. And cold, always cold, so very cold. Deathly cold.

Rushing...rushing...rushing.

Nowhere to go.

* * *

Annie lay lifeless, disoriented, yet encased in something warm and comfortable. She had a thought that this was what it must be like to be in the womb, and if this is what it was like, why did anyone ever want to come out? The sun pushed down on the back of her neck and she stretched her jaw. She sensed pain deep inside but chose to focus instead on her warm immobility. A sound entered the arena of her senses. It was familiar somehow. A crackling sound, intermittent, but then it stopped. Best not to worry about it and keep focusing on the warmth, she told herself. But no, the sound was back. Clattering, crackling. Maybe even like rattling. In fact, very much like rattling. Not good.

"It senses your body warmth," said a voice, that also sounded familiar. It was a relaxed, friendly voice, and Annie was glad it was there. "It's trying to figure out if it wants to eat you or you want to eat it."

Annie raised her head. She cracked open an eye.

Eli smiled. "I bet it figures you want to eat it."

Annie laid her head back down. "What happened?"

"Don't know," Eli said. "My guess is you were body surfing."

Annie raised her head again and smiled. Little by little it was coming back to her. Monroe, her father, the flash flood. It was looking pretty certain she was still alive.

"Not a good place for it though, Annie."

She pulled herself up to her knees. "The rattler?"

"He went off looking for a mouse. You were too big for him."

"Oh!" She felt a searing pain in her hip.

"Get a little dinged up, did you?" Eli helped her stand and brushed silt from her shoulders.

"The sheriff's deputies?"

"I saw them rushing up the mountain, but the flood carried you all the way down here. Seems the Great Spirit likes you."

"*Likes* me?" She wiped grit from her face.

"Well, so to speak."

She pulled open her pockets and gobs of wet sand and rocks fell out. She reached for the back of her waistband. "Uh, I had a pistol."

"The mountain has it now."

She nodded.

"Come on. I'll give you a lift. We have a shower you can use." He looked her over. "We've got a car wash too. Maybe we should run you through that first."

Annie laughed and they walked to a red pickup.

Eli drove her to his house in Apache Junction. His house really seemed more of a workshop, its three-car garage filled with all kinds of gear: pickaxes, coiled rope, flashlights, radios, neon safety vests. Annie asked about Thad, if Eli knew anything, and she breathed a sigh of relief to hear that Thad was still alive, albeit in Sheriff Delgado's lockup. Then all she could think about was Chase and getting back to him in Justiceburg. God—or the Great Spirit as Eli called it—only knew what she would do from there. One thing was sure though. Eli was seeming like a gift from this Great Spirit.

After her shower, Eli set Annie up with clothes, granted pretty different clothes—red calypso pants, a plaid top and cloth Converse high-tops—another pistol (he said he had "a bunch of them"), and a car she could use, a sky-blue El Camino that looked like it had been in a flash flood too, water-stained sandbags in the back. When Annie asked why he was being so kind, he said that Thad had told him to be nice to her because she was trying to do something good.

Annie gave him a hug, fired up the El Camino and headed for Justiceburg.

# Chapter Fifteen

Thad was alive, Annie thought as she drove to Justiceburg. He was alive. She had so much confidence in him, she was even hoping he could outsmart Sheriff Delgado and escape from the lockup. She frowned. Surely Delgado now had her phone, and with it the photographs of Chase incriminating Monroe. She shifted in her seat, her hip aching. Her whole body was aching actually. Oh well, she thought. She knew she was lucky to be alive and she was grateful for the kindness Eli had shown her. And she knew as long as she had Chase, there was a fighting chance things might work out. She stopped at the motel to pick up her belongings and headed back to the Salamander Beauty Salon.

Beatrice Parker wasn't there. Neither was Chase. Beatrice had left a number. Annie phoned from the salon and set up a meet at the Desert Hideaway motel on the outskirts of town. A million thoughts raced through Annie's mind as she drove there, most of them centering around the ten million reasons why Beatrice might have taken Chase out there.

The Desert Hideaway was a horseshoe-shaped motel alongside a state road. Only two cars were in the parking lot. An old man, remarkably in overalls and a long-sleeved sweatshirt in the heat, was sweeping a patio near the office. Annie drove straight to room #3E, hurried up the walk and knocked.

Beatrice swung the door open and before Annie could say a word spoke.

"I figured it out, Andrea." Beatrice shook her head apologetically. "I know faces. I study 'em. It's my stock in trade. And all the news programs started showing your photos, and you changing your color and cut so often it all just fell right into place."

Annie, her heart beating triple-time, saw Chase lying on the bed, looking toward her.

"I couldn't keep Frank at the Salamander. I was just too nervous. Like someone besides me would figure out what was going on…and…and…" Beatrice looked Annie in the eye. "…I wanted to hear your side of the story before I did anything."

Annie sighed and figured under the circumstances she had to tell her everything and let the chips fall where they may. So she did.

"I knew it!" Beatrice slapped her thigh. "Ha ha. You fooled Mr. Billionaire himself." She slapped her thigh again. "A kid scammed Mr. Macho Billionaire. Oh, it's just too precious."

Annie walked past Beatrice, sat on the bed and stroked Chase's forehead. He reached for her.

"Aww." Beatrice clasped her hands to her cheeks and smiled.

Annie felt all her pain disappear as Chase clutched her. Beatrice could do what she wanted but Annie was going to savor this moment, this love she felt from, and for Chase.

Beatrice looked her over. "Well, I must say that's a funky little outfit you've put together. I especially like the calypso pants."

Annie laughed. "Don't ask." Maybe this wouldn't be so bad after all.

Beatrice nodded, then she pulled on her lip. "What do you think our next step should be?"

*Our* next step? Annie thought. Was it possible Beatrice wasn't going to turn her in? Was it possible she was going to *help* her? "You'd really help me?"

"Heck, yeah. It'd be fun sticking it to Mr. Billionaire."

Annie was thrilled but also leery. It was pretty apparent Beatrice had a big chip on her shoulder against men. But with no other alternatives and Beatrice knowing the whole story she decided to go for it. "Well, I'd need to get the photos of Chase at Monroe's that are on my phone. The only problem is my phone is in Sheriff Delgado's lockup."

"Hmm."

"I know. It's a mess."

"Well, you know that lockup is hardly going to be Alcatraz, honey. I was married to a cop in Paradise Valley, and that jail wasn't much to speak of, nor quite frankly were their deputies, especially my ex." She grinned wickedly.

Annie eased in a long slow breath. "I do have an idea but… but I don't think I could pull it off myself."

Beatrice sat on the bed. "I'm all go, girlfriend. Spill the beans."

"Well…I'm worth ten million dollars to whoever turns me in." Annie laughed. "I would think that would be quite an incentive for a deputy to be a little lax in his duties and let one bit of evidence slip through the cracks, namely my phone, if he knew he could collect on me."

"Ah, I see what you're saying." Beatrice nodded. "Yes, I definitely see what you're saying. And, honey, chances are that deputy is not even going to know why that phone is there—they don't tell the deputies diddly-squat. He'll think it's no big deal."

"But why would a deputy think anyone would trade ten million dollars for a phone?"

Beatrice pursed her lips. "Hmm…I'll tell him there's naked pictures of us on it…" She grinned big. "…having sex!" She guffawed. "Guys are creeps, Andrea. Trust me, they'll love it—and fall for it. Well, one of them anyway."

* * *

Annie managed to anchor Chase's car seat in the middle of the El Camino's seat and they loaded the car up and headed for Sheriff Delgado's lockup.

Beatrice was saying they needed to find the cop bar—"there's usually only one"—near the lockup. That would be where the deputies hung. She explained that it was legal for anybody with a permit to bring a gun into a bar, but that cop bars really were like the Wild West. Drinking and guns were a bad enough mix, but drinking and guns and testosterone-fueled cops was well, mayhem. "There." She pointed. "That's got to be it."

Annie looked. A brown adobe building was half in the shadow of the setting sun. A faded sign said DOS COYOTES TAP and under that PACKAGE GOODS and COCKTAILS. Bars covered the windows, a bow-tie neon Budweiser sign in one of them. It was eight in the evening, still a fair amount of daylight left, but the parking lot was jammed. "Looks crowded for being so early."

Beatrice laughed. "Believe me, Andrea, the time means nothing to these dirtballs. When they're done with their shift they drink. Done at four in the afternoon, they drink. Done at six in the morning, they drink. The only time cop bars aren't full is when they're closed."

At least, Annie figured, the El Camino looked like it belonged in the lot full of pickups and Harleys. Annie had been in bars before but only for special occasion parties for friends or relatives. She'd never been in a cop bar. She didn't even know there were such places.

She went over her plan with Beatrice as they sat in the

parking lot, a few more bar patrons pulling up, slamming doors and heading in. Pumped up by resentment against her ex (her 'wusband' she called him) Beatrice was all for it.

Annie got the plan rolling. She had Beatrice take some photos of her and Chase with Tara's phone. Then the plan was for all three of them to go into the bar together, Annie just to use the bathroom, but to make herself very visible in the process of walking in and out. Then Beatrice would select some deputy (Beatrice swore she had 'cop-dar' and could pick out cops anywhere) and after a few drinks show him the photos of Annie and Chase and convince him to hand over Annie's phone in the lockup in exchange for turning Annie in for the ten million.

Annie was concerned. Beatrice was just too animated, too excited, too angry at men—but it was too late to turn back now. They headed for the bar. A lone wispy tree stood next to the bar entrance and looked out of place, anything natural seeming unfitting alongside the bar's man-made raunchiness. Just before they got to the door, Annie, sunglass-less, Chase in her arms, turned to Beatrice. "If you can, find out about Thad too."

Well, this was definitely no normal bar, Annie thought walking in. Rock music blasting on an actual jukebox in the corner. The wall behind the bar was made up of rows of bottles of every sort of alcohol imaginable. The place reeked of smoke, even though smoking was prohibited. Annie felt self-conscious being so young and doubly self-conscious about having Chase in her arms, but it helped when the blonde bartender—a thirty-something woman in tight, frayed blue jeans and a bare midriff Tecate t-shirt—smiled at her. Annie forced herself to walk as slowly as she could and make eye contact all around. *Look at me*, she was thinking as she passed amongst what must have been cops, in their jeans and tight t-shirts. After what seemed an eternity she got to the bathroom.

She locked the door behind her and Chase and checked herself in the mirror. She still wasn't used to seeing herself with the buzz cut of black hair. The bathroom was guy-ish, just a stand-sink and a toilet, the seat up, the water in the bowl still swirling a bit. Chase, remarkably considering the rock music blasting, wasn't crying, and seemed happy just to be with her.

A knock on the door.

"Un-huh, be right out," Annie called. A deep breath and then to Chase, "All right, little man, here we go again."

Slowly, hopefully naturally, she made her way back through the bar. She got a nice smile from a cocktail waitress, but the men's glares felt like lustful hooks, making her so uncomfortable. Again it seemed to take an interminably long time but she made it outside, the air there still powerfully warm, the last of the setting sun glinting off the storefronts across the street.

She, Chase next to her in the car seat, settled in the El Camino. Now all that was left was to wait.

Two hours later a tipsy Beatrice came out and piled in. "It's all set, girlfriend. Clay—my new *friend...*" she said with an eye-widening smirk. "...is working seven-to-three tomorrow at the lockup. He told me we're good to go. And let me tell ya, Andrea, this guy's a real piece of work." She shook her head and looked angry enough to spit. "He was already groping me in there." She took a deep breath. "And, yeah, he said Thad's there too."

# Chapter Sixteen

The next morning, Annie packed up Chase and all their things from the motel, picked up Beatrice, and drove them to Delgado's lockup. Annie was thinking Beatrice sounded awfully confident about the plan to get Annie's phone back. Like she did this sort of thing all the time. But Beatrice's men-anger was still smoldering too. It was disconcerting.

"Men are so easy to fool," Beatrice railed. "It's embarrassing."

Chase had had a rough night. Something hadn't been sitting right with him, and he was still cranky, but besides that, all Annie could think about was Thad. Thad and those deep brown eyes of his, that wise face, his mysteriousness—and how much trouble he was in because of her.

Just before they got to the lockup Beatrice ran over what she was planning on doing. She'd go into the lockup under the guise of claiming she'd been robbed. Deputy Clay would take her statement and then slip her a plastic bag with Annie's phone in it. Then Beatrice would give Deputy Clay the address where he could find Annie. One thing Annie didn't like was Beatrice (she'd discovered it in the glove compartment) insisting on taking the pistol into the lockup with her. Beatrice said everybody in Arizona carried guns and she might need it as a backup.

The station, besides the American flag and the POLICE sign over the door, looked like just about any other Arizona public building: an orange tile roof, beige sandstone walls, bushes out front, meticulously trimmed. Annie kept thinking about Thad being in there. She wondered what he'd been charged with. If he'd been treated well. God, she'd love to see him and knowing he was so close she longed for him. But enough of that now. This was too important. She had to be sharp. Beatrice told her to keep the car running and walked quickly into the station.

"Oh, Chase," Annie said, gazing at him in the car seat next to her. "Such a big commotion you're causing everyone." Life had seemed a dream, more of a nightmare actually, these last few days. But gazing into Chase's eyes and feeling the affection, the gratitude coming from him filled her with immense joy and a powerful feeling of love. When she looked up, Beatrice, pistol in hand, was running from the police station. She hopped into the El Camino.

"Let's go!"

Annie threw the car into gear. "What happened?"

"Go go go!"

Annie could smell smoke. Could it be from the pistol? She hit the gas. "Beatrice, what happened?"

Beatrice frowned and checked behind them. "The jerk messed me up."

"How?"

"He didn't want to give me your damn phone. He was looking for the naked pictures of us on it, and when he didn't find them, he got suspicious."

"So you didn't get it?" Annie floored the car onto the highway.

"Oh, I got it all right." Beatrice laughed and kept checking behind her. "But I had to ruffle a few feathers."

Oh God. What did that mean? "Beatrice?"

"Good thing you gave me that gun."

Annie's heart sunk. She drew in a long breath. "Beatrice, did you shoot him?"

Beatrice frowned again. "I shot *at* him. I don't know if I hit him."

"Oh my God."

"He wouldn't give me the damn phone! Here!" She handed the phone over. "But fortunately…" She laughed. "…the gun and the look in my eye made him change his mind. Which was all well and good, but then as I was leaving, he pulled his gun so I had to fire a few times to get out of there."

"So you might have shot him."

"I told you I had to do it." She punched the dash.

Beatrice suddenly seemed like a crazy person. Annie didn't feel Chase was safe being with her. *She* didn't feel safe being with her. She sighed. "All right. So let me have the gun."

Beatrice checked over her shoulder yet again. "No, I'm gonna hang on to it for a minute."

Annie's heart raced.

* * *

Annie drove them back to the Desert Hideaway motel. Swamped with cops. She drove to the Salamander Beauty Salon. Ditto. Beatrice was making her more and more nervous, going on and on about how this Deputy Clay had 'betrayed' her and 'deserved what he got.' It was clear to Annie that if she was going to have any chance at all of saving Chase, they were going to have to get away from Beatrice. But how? Not wanting to get Beatrice any more wound up than she already was, Annie asked her, "So what do you think we should do?"

Beatrice shrugged. "There's only one thing *to* do—head north."

"Like Sedona?"

Beatrice shook her head. “No, north-north. Canada north. That’s the only chance I got now.”

Annie blinked a few times. “But you said you just shot *at* him. Maybe it won’t be so bad if you turn yourself in.”

Beatrice reached over Chase and grabbed Annie’s arm. “Not gonna happen, girlfriend!”

“Beatrice, let go.”

She did but with a shove.

“Beatrice, I can’t go to Canada.”

“Why not?”

“I just can’t. I’ve got the baby—”

“And you’ve got the phone and the photos and you can put them on the Internet in Canada.”

Annie bit her lip. “It’s not that simple. I put the photos on the Internet before and they did nothing.”

Beatrice flipped on the radio and scowled. “So you lied to me?”

“I didn’t *lie*.” Annie could hear the panic in her voice. “Getting the photos was critical, was absolutely necessary, but it was also just the start.”

“Ah.” Beatrice nodded. “I get it. I helped you and now you won’t help me. So you’re one of those, are you?”

It wasn’t worth answering her. Beatrice was obviously very disturbed. Annie looked at the gas gauge. It was getting low. Chase needed his bottle, and she was nearly out of his formula. “I asked you for help. You agreed.”

“But now I’m asking you and you won’t help me.”

“Not won’t, Beatrice. Can’t.”

“I know you,” Beatrice said with more nods. “I know your type—little rich girl from the valley.” She spun the dial on the radio and stopped on an all-news station.

"Another update," an announcer said, "on the cop killer who gunned down Deputy Clay Stanhouse at Sheriff Delgado's lockup earlier today. She is said to have escaped with an accomplice in a blue station wagon."

Annie could feel the sweat coming up on her brow. Cop killer.

"Well, well, well." Beatrice narrowed her eyes. "I guess I hit that old boy after all. Can't say he didn't have it coming."

Annie shut the radio.

Beatrice switched it back on. "Canada, here we come."

"Beatrice, I have no money."

"Relax, I've got MasterCard." She tapped her purse.

"I have to stop for gas."

Beatrice leaned over and looked at the gauge. "No you don't. You've got a quarter tank."

"I have to go to the bathroom."

"Pull to the side of the road then, valley girl. Find a bush like the rest of us."

Annie swerved onto the shoulder, the sudden movement startling Chase, starting him crying.

Beatrice laughed. "See what you did."

Annie calmed Chase and got out. Clenching her fists she headed into the desert. Beatrice killed a cop. Beatrice was crazy. And now Chase was going to pay for it. Annie didn't have to go to the bathroom but she squatted behind a bush to buy time to think. She looked around. Nothing but scruffy desert—sagebrush, cacti, spindly cholla and of course rocks. Red rocks. Annie was so angry at Beatrice she felt like *she* was getting red. Rocks. Red rocks. She picked one up. It was the size of a baseball. She looked at Beatrice in the El Camino. At the cop killer Beatrice. And who knew, maybe Beatrice would kill Chase too. Maybe directly, maybe indirectly by forcing him back to Monroe.

She hefted the rock. Beatrice was staring at the radio, as if trying to extract something from it with her eyes. It was a terrible thought Annie had. It brought up bile in her throat. And yet…and yet. If it would save Chase.

She held the rock behind her back and walked to the El Camino, the pressure mounting. Beatrice might kill Chase. Beatrice had to be stopped. Annie bypassed the driver's-side door and walked around car's flat open bed. She swallowed hard and blinked a few times before she got to the passenger-side window.

Beatrice looked up. "You done yet?"

Annie smacked her on the side of the head with the rock. Beatrice went down, her torso thrust toward the driver's side. Annie stood back and dropped the rock. She was shaking. *My God, what have I done?*

Only the sound of Chase's crying drew her back into reality. Beatrice lay slumped on top of him.

Annie lugged the dead-weight Beatrice off Chase. Had she killed her? Annie's breathing quickened, her heart fluttered. Was she a murderer? She put her ear to Beatrice's mouth. Thank God—she was breathing. Annie shut the radio and comforted Chase but what now? First things first. She grabbed the pistol from Beatrice's purse and put it back in the El Camino's glove compartment. Cars were going by, some slowing. This was rural Arizona after all—people stopped to help. What would she tell them? She sighed. Oh, she wasn't sure what to do but knew for damn sure she didn't want Beatrice riding in front with them. She glanced in the back bed of the El Camino. There were a few sandbags. Okay. She could deal with that.

She checked for traffic. A grain truck went by, slowing, its driver peering over. Annie gave him a thumbs-up and the truck passed. Then she popped open the passenger-side door and pulled Beatrice from the car, the stylist's feet dragging on the dusty shoulder. Now the hard part. She stood Beatrice up against the car, then crouched low, grabbed her by the knees and lugged her over the edge of the El Camino's bed, Beatrice thudding in. Annie jumped into the bed and dragged Beatrice so her back was to the window separating the bed from the cab. The idea was to make it look like she was joy riding back there, so Annie dragged a sandbag onto her lap to prop her up. Oh no. An SUV was slowing. Annie jumped out of the bed, hopped into the driver's side and turned the ignition. The SUV pulled onto the shoulder. Annie waved to its driver and stepped on the gas, gravel spitting, dual shoots of dust rising, as she roared back onto the road. With the news report—thank God it said the killer had escaped in a station wagon and not an El Camino—there was no time to waste.

A host of electrical towers were on her right, a rutty dirt road leading to them. She turned onto the road. The El Camino handled the ruts well, rocking a bit, but powering through. Annie swung the car around, Beatrice listing a little, and far enough from the road to not be seen, she got out, straightened Beatrice and lugged a couple more sandbags across her lap to secure her. Now she needed to get her to a hospital.

On the highway she headed back south for the valley. She needed a stretch where no cars or trucks would pass her and see Beatrice. She swallowed. A fiery red Corvette, top down, was flying up on her. Oh well, at least the Corvette was a good deal lower and it blew by. Trucks, Annie was thinking. Eighteen wheelers sitting up high would be the problem. But so far so good.

She checked on Chase. He was okay. The little guy was calming. It seemed that whenever he was alone with her he was okay.

She checked the rear view mirror for cars or trucks. Wait a minute. Wait a minute. Was Beatrice moving? Or it could have been her imagination. Annie had to keep her eyes on the road. It was only a two-lane highway, cars, semis flying past her coming the other way as she sped along. She checked again. Oh my God, oh no, Beatrice was stirring.

She was struggling to get out from under the sandbags. Annie glanced at Chase. She didn't want to stop. If she pulled over and motorists stopped to help, it could only mean trouble. But oh, Beatrice was climbing toward the passenger-side window. Annie looked at the glove compartment. The gun was in there but what was she going to do—shoot Beatrice as she crawled through the window? Annie shook her head. She'd already figured she'd killed her once. She yelled, "Stay back there!"

Beatrice's fingers were gripping the door frame. Yes, she was going to try and pull herself into the car! "Beatrice, you're going to kill yourself!"

Beatrice's head was in the car now. "No! I'm going to kill *you!*"

Annie reached across, the El Camino drifting onto the shoulder, opened the glove compartment and grabbed the gun. "Don't make me use this, Beatrice! Because I will!" She aimed the pistol right between Beatrice's eyes.

"So shoot, valley girl." Beatrice tumbled onto the passenger-side floor. Chase started crying.

Oh God. Annie double checked that Chase was strapped tightly in the car seat, and when Beatrice righted herself, Annie slammed on the brakes, Beatrice flying headfirst into the dash, her body recoiling back onto the seat. She was out cold.

* * *

Annie used Tara's phone to find the nearest hospital, then raced the unconscious Beatrice there. A wheelchair sat outside the emergency room doors and Annie plopped Beatrice onto it. Then she drove to the far edge of the hospital lot and watched till a woman emerged. The woman went back into the emergency room and two nurses ran out and wheeled Beatrice in. Annie took off.

She hoped Beatrice was all right. Of course she did. Beatrice had been decent, helpful. Annie marveled that anyone would resist the temptation to turn her in for the ten million. But Beatrice had also been a huge threat to Chase—and she'd killed a cop.

Annie headed back to the valley. She looked over at Chase as she drove, and beyond him saw Beatrice's blood on the seat. Annie could hardly believe she'd hit Beatrice with the rock, then slammed on the brakes the way she had, sending her into the dash. She really could've killed her. When she stopped for gas, she called the hospital to check on her, saying she was her sister. A nurse told her Beatrice was going to be okay.

Back on the road, Annie was going seventy-five in a sixty zone. She put her foot on the brake. If she got pulled over with the blood on the seat, they were done for, whether or not the cop recognized her.

For once Annie had no plan. She was feeling like the bacteria she'd studied in Mr. Jankowski's biology class. She was just clinging to other organisms and mutating. Then the bacteria either thrived or died off. She had a moment when she wondered if she was headed for the latter end. But one thing was sure—she wasn't giving up because she had to keep Chase safe.

Tara's phone beeped that it had received a text. Annie checked it.

*We know u know where Rebarchek is Tara. You can tell us or we'll make u tell us. Yur choice baby kidnapper's friend.*

It was from Henry Buck, quarterback of the Alameda High football team and premier jerk.

Annie texted Tara. She arranged to meet her friend at the park with the ponds.

# Chapter Seventeen

A host of insects hovered over the park's ponds in the early evening sunlight. Inline skaters, bicyclists and women with baby strollers dotted the multi-purpose path even though it still had to be ninety-five. Annie, sunglasses on, Chase in her arms, baby bag slung over her shoulder, approached the bench where Tara sat staring at a phone.

"Tara, thanks for coming." Annie sat down next to her friend.

"Annie? Is that you?"

Annie nodded.

"Oh wow. Your hair. I mean, I recognize your voice but that's about it."

Annie was thinking *good*. "Although I'd love to I don't want to take a lot of time here, Tara. You saw the text from Buck?"

"Yeah, what a jerk that bonehead is. I told you about him and his idiot jock friends."

"But it was a threat."

Tara swallowed. "Yeah."

Annie touched her friend's hand. "I've got to believe that this whole thing is going to be over soon."

Tara leaned over to look at Chase. "He looks better, Annie. Since he's been with you."

Annie smiled. "Yeah?"

"Absolutely."

"Tara, are you going to be okay with Buck and the jocks?"

"Buck's an idiot."

"Even so, if you want to bail I'll understand."

An inline skater, a teenager with a floppy-eared hat, whizzed by. “Hey!”

Annie laughed. “You know him?”

Tara nodded. “He’s in my fourth period algebra. He’s geeky but he’s cool.”

“So yeah, if you want to bail—”

“I’m not bailing, but what are you thinking about doing now?”

“Thanks.” Annie hugged her friend. “Well, I was thinking that since everybody wants the ten million, why not have a contest to see who gets me?”

Tara shrugged. “What do you mean?”

“Just put a contest on Twitter, Facebook, Instagram, anywhere you can think, that there will be a contest to see who gets to turn me in for the ten million.”

“What kind of a contest?”

“I’ll leave that up to you, Tara. You’re the social platform whiz. Just flood all your followers and see what happens. Do it for this Saturday. That should be enough time to gather momentum. Yeah, make it for Saturday at Terahawk Peak at noon.”

“You realize that I’m going to draw a lot of attention setting it up?”

“Yeah.”

“And a lot of people might think it’s a hoax?”

“I admit it could be a mess.”

Tara rested her hands on her thighs.

A bike patrol cop rolled down the path.

Annie, sweating, especially with the pistol in the baby bag, whispered, “Just act natural.”

“I always act natural. That’s part of my charm.” Tara smiled at the cop and he nodded to her.

Annie exhaled deeply as he passed.

"See, he was nice."

"Yeah."

"And I gotta believe a lot of these cops, Annie, really, people in general, are going to be nice, are going to be on your side once they know how Monroe abused Chase."

"That's what I'm hoping the contest will do."

* * *

Annie borrowed all Tara's cash, twelve dollars. Tara left, and once again Annie had nowhere to go. The contest. Annie sat alone for a few minutes by the pond in the park and pondered the contest. Kids were playing with battery-operated boats, the boats' whiny buzzing filling the air. From the condos behind the park came the smell of barbecue. People were crazy for contests. And ten million dollars to the winner. If that wasn't enough incentive, nothing was. She remembered her father being so excited when the golf tournament, the Fed Ex Cup, was created featuring a ten million dollar prize. And she liked the idea of her contest taking place at Terahawk Peak. Terahawk Peak was familiar and she felt comfortable there. She hugged her waist. What exactly the contest would be, well, that would be up to Tara, but she knew Tara, a social dynamo, would come up with something great. The kids gave up on the boats, the park suddenly quiet. Annie exhaled. She had to go somewhere. She headed for the El Camino.

Seeing the El Camino reminded her of Eli, and she remembered Thad had said that when things settled down she ought to contact Eli again. And if anybody knew what was happening with Thad it would be Eli. She headed for Apache Junction as the sun was setting. Again, she was careful to obey the speed limit. She'd seen on TV how hard-core criminals are stopped for petty traffic violations, then arrested when the cops discover their serious crimes. No, she had to be super careful.

She was excited about seeing Eli, and excited to be, hopefully, finding out about Thad.

Fortunately, Eli was in his garage, working. Annie gathered Chase in her arms and weaved through the cars in the driveway, calling Eli's name.

Eli set down a knife he was sharpening and walked to the garage's apron. He smiled. "Just couldn't stay away from the place, huh?"

Annie felt the tension in her neck and shoulders melt. She felt like she was drawing in Eli's peace by osmosis. She wanted to say *thank you* but said, "Yep, Apache Junction's a magnet."

"Well." He nodded, his ponytails on either side sliding up and down his chest. "We're glad to have you, and the little fellow too." He looked at Chase, then headed back into the garage. "Yes," he said, and he pulled two deck chairs off hooks and brought them back to the apron. "Rest your weary bones for a minute."

They sat. It was a clear evening, finally cooling off enough to be comfortable, stars emerging in the immense blue-going-purple sky.

Annie stroked Chase's cheek. "Thanks, Eli."

He nodded. "It's a lot of responsibility for a young girl."

Annie smiled and the reality of that came home to her. Before this, her biggest life challenge had been deciding where to apply to college. She gazed at Chase. "This little guy keeps me going."

"It's a good thing you're doing."

Annie nodded. "Thanks, but sometimes I feel like I'm further from getting Chase out of this mess than ever before."

He smiled. "Life is often like that."

"Like what?"

"Things have to get worse before they get better."

Annie shrugged. "But why would that be?"

"Don't know. It just seems to be the way the Great Spirit works. Maybe he wants to test your courage, your determination."

"Oh my!" A gigantic orange moon was creeping over the summit of Superstition Mountain. "So beautiful!"

"The Great Spirit is an artist."

Annie took a deep breath. All this Great Spirit stuff was sounding so mysterious. "Seems to me like you've got a direct link to this Great Spirit, do you?"

Eli shook his head. "No, the Great Spirit shows glimpses of how it works. I just pay attention."

"So how does it work?"

The moon, immense, its dark patches vivid against the bright orange, continued to rise from behind the mountain like a night sun.

"In many ways."

"But how does it work pertaining to me and Chase and Thad?"

Eli shrugged. "When people want to do good the Great Spirit provides a way."

Annie laughed. "Well, with all due respect, Eli, the Great Spirit isn't doing such a great job of providing a way in our case."

Eli nodded. "It's early. You're young."

"Just amazing," Annie said, her mouth falling open a little as she looked back at the moon, tossing its orange light to the earth, the driveway, the cars' moonshadows falling long onto the dusty front yard. All that beauty combined with what Eli was saying, Annie felt as if she was being swept up into a mystical state. It scared her, the fear racing around her stomach.

"Don't be afraid," Eli said.

"What?" Was he reading her mind? Who was this man? "Who are you? What do you do?"

He smiled. "I'm Eli. I'm a helicopter pilot for Apache Junction Search and Rescue."

He seemed more like a holy man to Annie. She took several deep breaths to steady herself. "Okay."

"I pluck people off the mountain. People who underestimate the mountain's power. They get trapped or fall and break a leg."

Annie was settling down. "What about Thad, Eli? Sheriff Delgado has him."

Eli jutted his chin out. "Sheriff Delgado is no match for the Great Spirit."

"But Delgado is evil. He's sadistic."

Eli nodded. "He's still no match for the Great Spirit."

Annie smiled.

"Thad has committed no crime. And the owner of the *Superstition Mountain Independent* went to high school with the governor. She's calling in a favor."

"So he'll be released?"

"A tragedy at Delgado's lockup…"

Annie groaned, remembering Beatrice killing the deputy.

"…is slowing things down."

Annie nodded. A phone beeped. It was a text from Tara.

*Had to borrow Kristen's phone, Annie. Henry Buck stole mine. He's seen our texts. Annie, the phone you're holding has GPS tracking activated. Get rid of it ASAP!!! Buck's coming for you!!!*

# Chapter Eighteen

Annie jumped up from the deck chair. She apologized to Eli for leaving so abruptly, and she tried to take Eli's calm with her. It didn't work.

She didn't know how much time she had before Henry Buck and the jocks would be on her and Chase, and she didn't want to ditch the phone right near Eli's. But where to dump it in a place that would get them off her scent? She drove onto the highway heading west and exited in Gilbert. She saw a lumber yard that's parking lot was nearly empty. She drove to the light pole in the center of the lot, pitched Tara's phone and tore out of there.

On her way out of the lot four muscle cars—one she recognized as Henry Buck's—poured in. They blazed toward the center of the lot. Annie, still concerned about getting stopped for speeding, had to take a chance and put the pedal to the floor, the El Camino rocketing back to the highway.

With one eye glued to the rear view mirror for the jocks she headed for Glendale and Monroe's 'wife's,' Vivian Sanchez's, apartment. She was thinking that up to this point everything she'd tried to help Chase hadn't worked, and she figured it was mainly because she was a seventeen-year-old high school kid and it was her word again superstar billionaire environmentalist Houston Monroe's. But if she had Sanchez's voice added to hers, the media would have to pay attention, and if she had Chase with her when she visited, Sanchez would probably be more amenable to lending her support.

Thank goodness Chase napped in the El Camino on the ride over. The last thing she needed was him colicky. And oh, it had been challenging enough visiting Sanchez's apartment during the day without Chase. Now, well, she would just have to take her chances.

At least this time she knew where she was going. When she got there and parked she put the pistol in the baby bag—why not, she figured. She climbed from the car, threw the baby bag over her shoulder, and with Chase in her arms approached the apartment building made up of seemingly thousands of balconies, a little world on each, some with boom boxes blasting, others with smoke drifting from barbecue grills. She pulled open the thick metal door to the lobby and as soon as she did she remembered she'd have to climb seven flights to get to the apartment. Seven flights with Chase in her arms.

She gritted her teeth and started up the stifling hot staircase smelling of curry. Oh, she thought, this place needs open windows. At least Chase was being good. As usual, he seemed happy just to be with her, which was a good feeling for Annie too. She hadn't really had the chance to think about it, but when the time came, it was going to be so hard to give him up. So hard.

Huffing and puffing, sweating, Chase feeling stuck to her skin, they made it to the seventh floor. "We did it!"

Annie walked down the hall, stood outside the door to 739, dabbed the perspiration from Chase's brow, then wiped her own face. She cleared her throat and knocked.

"Yes?"

"Vivian, it's Annie Rebarchek."

"Oh!" Silence.

"Vivian."

"Give me just a second here, Annie. I'm not dressed."

Annie frowned. This suddenly wasn't feeling so right.

Something in Vivian's voice sounded off. "Vivian."

The door opened. Vivian, in a pink slit skirt, strap sandals and a silk blouse, stood aside and waved them in. "So this is the little guy, huh?" she said. Once they were in, she quickly triple locked the door behind them.

Annie knew Vivian had just lied about not being dressed. No way she'd gotten this decked out that fast. Still Annie couldn't put her finger on what was wrong. "Vivian, this feels bad somehow. I came here to ask for your support but now the whole vibe feels terrible."

Vivian looked away.

"Please tell me what's going on."

The pretty Latina sighed. Finally, she nodded toward a cell phone on a cocktail table. "They're on their way."

"*Who's* on their way?" Annie pulled Chase close.

Vivian bit her bottom lip and looked down. "Everyone."

Annie grabbed her arm. "Who?"

"Monroe, Delgado, his deputies."

Annie turned to go. Now Vivian grabbed her.

"Take your hands off me!"

"Just stay here, Annie. If you leave, they'll kill you. Monroe hates you. He wants you dead, and Delgado's an animal who will do anything Monroe says. But if you stay here, I'm a witness. They won't be able to hurt you."

Annie pursed her lips. "Why? Why'd you do it, Vivian? He's just an innocent baby."

Vivian's chin sunk to her chest.

Annie started undoing the deadbolts.

"Don't, Annie! They'll shoot you!"

Annie unfastened the last deadbolt. She stared at Vivian.

"He's just an innocent baby," she said again and walked out.

She headed for the stairwell but heard voices, hurried footfalls coming up. She ran back the other way. Vivian was leaning out her door. Annie grabbed the pistol from the baby bag and pointed it at her. Vivian disappeared behind her slammed door. It would be just seconds till whoever was in the stairwell arrived.

Annie knocked on a door with a little tri-color Mexican flag on it.

A gray-haired lady in a floral house dress and slippers opened the door. "*Si?*"

Oh God. Annie remembered a little from Mr. Kingsbury's Spanish class. "*Puedo entrar?* Can I come in?"

The woman shrugged. "*Por que?*"

Why? Annie was on the verge of fainting—the stairwell door about to open. "*Tengo un problema con mi bebe.* I have a problem with my baby."

The woman looked at Chase. She looked at Annie. She nodded them in.

White carpeting but not wall to wall. A bookcase, only a handful of books in it. A table covered with a blue and white check table cloth, and a young boy sitting at it playing a video game.

Annie was nearly hyperventilating. "*Ingles?*" she said. "Does anyone speak English?"

The woman nodded toward the boy. "Felipe?"

The boy, maybe ten, disappointed to be drawn away from his game looked up. "What?"

Annie went to him. "Felipe, my baby and I need to get out of here right away."

The boy shrugged.

"But we can't use the stairs."

"Why not?"

Annie frowned. She had to go for broke. "The police are after us."

The boy's eyes widened. "Why, what did you do?"

"Nothing." Annie shook her head. There was no time. Delgado's deputies would be knocking on the door any second. "It's a case of mistaken identity."

"Why don't you just tell them then?"

"Because they're bad men. Look, Felipe, is there any other way of getting out of here?"

He smiled. "I know of one way." Then he gave the old woman a wary look.

"What is it?" Annie cried.

"But it's no good for you."

"Well, what is it? We have no time."

He walked to a sliding glass door, pulled it open and stepped out onto a fire escape. He turned to look at Annie. She followed. "They don't keep it up," he said, peering down. "Steps missing. Railings rusty." He looked back into the apartment to make sure the old woman was out of earshot. "I've gone down it though."

Annie looked down. Her head swirled. Her gut churned. The fire escape was rusted wrought iron, warped bars for steps, potted plants and drying laundry crowding the landings. She stepped onto the first rung and the ball of her foot rolled on it. With Chase in her arms this would be a nightmare. She stepped back.

The boy shut the sliding door, as if to make sure the old woman didn't hear what he was about to say. Annie was guessing the woman was his grandmother. He said, "I could help you."

Annie nodded.

The boy disappeared into the apartment. He reappeared with a backpack. “Put the baby in here and I’ll guide you down.”

Annie thought of the alternative. Monroe. Delgado. She grabbed the backpack, went back into the apartment and said to the old woman, “*Por favor?*” The old woman smiled and Annie handed Chase to her.

Annie tested the backpack’s straps. She tried it on her front. There was no way she was wearing it on her back. Satisfied it would work, she smiled and took Chase from the old woman, turned to Felipe and said, “Let’s go.”

The boy said to the old woman: *“Abuela, que es una emergencia. Tengo que ayudar a la mujer ya su bebe de escape de los hombres malos.”*

The woman frowned but nodded.

Annie said to her, “*Muchas gracias*.”

They went out on the balcony and Annie asked, “What did you say to her?”

“I told her you were a criminal.”

“Really?”

“Nah.” He laughed. “All right. I’m going to go first, and I’ll tell you what to look out for.”

Annie settled Chase into the backpack, now a frontpack, snug against her. He wasn’t going anywhere. “Okay.”

Step by shaky step they descended, Felipe offering up little warnings. “This one the railing on the right is broken. Don’t lean on it.” Annie was dripping sweat. Her hands were grimy with soot and rusty flakes but they were doing it.

They’d made it down three flights, only four to go, when Annie’s foot broke through a step. “Oh!” Chase was thrust forward into the steps, and right away she pushed back to look at him. He was okay. The backpack had protected him, but the jarring started him crying.

Felipe called up, "You're heavier than me so that one broke. That's the worst stretch though. You'll be okay the rest of the way."

Annie's shin throbbed but she was grateful Chase was okay.

Felipe was good to his word. He yanked down a ladder from the last landing and steadied it as Annie climbed down.

"Oh my God," Annie said when she put her feet on firm ground. She looked at Felipe. "Thank you."

"Yep. I didn't really think you were going to make it but you did."

Annie laughed, grateful he didn't tell her that on the way down. But now, she was thinking, she was still up against it—there was no way to get the El Camino, which was out front, where Delgado's deputies were no doubt swarming.

Felipe sensed her hesitation. "What are you going to do now?"

Annie frowned. "I need my car but it's in front and chances are there'll be cops all over the place."

The boy put a hand to his chin. "I can get it for you."

Annie looked at him. "Are you serious?"

"Is it a stick?"

Annie shook her head.

"I can get it then. What kind of car?"

"Well, El Camino."

"Oh, those are so cool. Give me the keys."

It was insane but it was an easy decision because she had no other options. She pinched a key, letting the others in the ring dangle, and handed it over.

# Chapter Nineteen

Oh my God. The kid pulled it off. The El Camino came rolling into the back parking lot. Annie gave Felipe a big hug and he smiled. Then she drove out the back, and when she got to the main road she saw cop cars everywhere in front, their lights flashing, a crowd of people gawking at the perimeter. Chase was okay. That was the main thing. She'd taken him out of the backpack and examined his little body from head to toe. But how crazy was this all getting? The emotional tension drained her. It wasn't that late but she was feeling like all she had strength left for was to get Chase and herself to another out of the way motel and crash. She headed for a motel she remembered seeing at the base of the South Mountains.

This was the sticks at least, she thought as she drove down a deserted desert road toward the massive South Mountains, which rimmed the south valley. To her right were penned cages filled with animals she couldn't quite identify. Then there was a light and she could see better. They were ostriches. She shrugged. She hadn't even known they had ostriches there. The once or twice she'd driven with her father in this area it had been mostly cotton fields, little white fluffy balls looking like marshmallows on green stalks, but the fields were too dark to see now, even with the moonlight. It got darker out here, she thought, than in the city, shouldered by the South Mountains and absence of city lights. There. She saw some lights up ahead on the right.

A wigwam was out front. Okay, it was just for decorative purposes. Now here was a big green WIGWAM LODGE neon sign, and next to it in red OFFICE. She pulled under an overhang. She left the car there—there were no other cars around—gathered up Chase and walked into the office. A little sign on the counter read FREE WI-FI. Another nice thing she was realizing was that people were usually really kind to her because of Chase. The motel clerk, a rail-thin woman in her forties with a peaceful face, asked over and over if there was anything else she could do. It was terribly sweet and especially nice after the nerve-wracking experience of climbing down the rickety fire escape.

Registered, Annie climbed back into the El Camino and drove to room 11. She collected Chase's things into the baby bag, shaking her head when she realized she still had the pistol in it, picked up Chase and headed for the room.

Someone was standing at the door. It was dark and the person was shadowy. All she could see was the top of his head and that just barely. She froze. Had she finally run out of luck? Well. She clutched Chase tight. If the person had tracked her down this far, he'd probably be able to track her anywhere. She might as well face the worst of it right away. She walked to the door.

She angled her head to see better. She squinted. Her breathing quickened. "Thad?"

Thad walked to her, embracing her and Chase.

"Oh my God," Annie said. "Is it really you?"

"It's me all right."

She held on to him. And held on to him. She took a deep breath and sighed it out. "Oh, I'm so glad you're okay." She shook her head. "When I left that high school parking lot I didn't even know if they'd shot you."

Thad nodded. "It was a pretty dicey situation."

"So." She touched his cheek. "We should go in, huh?"

Another nod. "Here, let me take him."

She handed him Chase, opened the door and flicked on the light. The room was pleasant. Pastel green walls, a little table with blue chairs and a queen-size bed with a green spread and white, very clean-looking pillows set up against the headboard. She took Chase back and laid him on the bed. She turned to Thad. “So.”

He smiled. “So.”

It hit her. It was just him and her. Alone together. It had been so long since she’d had such thoughts, such feelings. She just wanted to inhale him, not sexually, but she wanted to grasp his body within hers and never let him go. “So,” she said again.

“So.”

She felt herself to be blushing. “So…how did you get out of Delgado’s lockup?”

“My boss had a friend in high places.”

She remembered Eli telling her that. “Okay. Next question. How did you find me?”

He nodded. “Eli has tracking devices in all his vehicles—in case they’re stolen.”

“I see.” She desperately needed a shower and sleep but she needed this even more. She stepped to him, laid her head on his chest and felt his arms surround her. “I missed you.”

“Yep. Missed you too.”

She wanted to kiss him but knew if she did they wouldn’t stop and there were things they needed to do first. “Thad, I actually got my phone out of Delgado’s lockup so now you can send the photos of Chase to your Peace Corps contact, right?”

“Now how in the world did you manage to get your phone out of the lockup?”

She shook her head. “I’ll tell you later, but you can get the pics out?”

"Absolutely. Let me grab something from my car first and I'll be right back."

He ran out into the night while Annie looked for her phone in the baby bag. Where was it now? She remembered Beatrice giving it to her. She dug through baby wipes, towels and formula. There was the pistol but no phone. Okay. She opened a side pocket zipper and there it was. Thank God.

Thad walked in with a laptop and set it up on the little table. "Don't go online yet. I can do something to encrypt it."

"Okay." She powered up her phone. She unlocked the keypad, hit the menu button and toggled to the photos folder. She clicked it. PHOTO FOLDER EMPTY. She felt like she was seeing things. She backed out of the folder and tried again. Same result. "Thad?"

He had a cord running from the laptop, the screen materializing, the Microsoft theme sounding. "Yeah?"

"The photos aren't there."

He rushed to her side. "You sure?"

She went through the toggling again. "Positive."

"Oh man."

She sat down on the bed next to Chase. "I don't get it. Why would they erase them?"

Thad frowned. "I should've seen that coming, Annie. They erased them because they *were* incriminating. Really, if you think about it, why would they keep them around?"

"Delgado is that much in Monroe's pocket?"

"Worse."

Annie sighed and lay back on the bed.

"Annie?"

She shook her head.

"Annie, I've got to go." He shut the laptop.

"Already?" She sprung up.

"I'm free but it was hell getting away from Delgado's surveillance. The longer I'm with you, the greater the chance they'll find me—and you and Chase."

She went to him. "I really want you to stay."

He took her in his arms.

She hugged him. "You sure you can't? Somehow? Some way?"

He smiled. "I can stay a little while."

She hugged him all the tighter and nodded. "I've got to take a quick shower. Will you watch Chase?"

"Of course."

She hurried to the shower. Oh, the warm gentle spray revived her. And how nice to have someone else—a man she trusted—helping with Chase. As she showered, it hit her again that she and Thad were alone together, and the loving thoughts and feelings and anticipation resurfaced. She towel dried her hair and dressed in her calypso pants and plaid top, leaving off her bra and the high-tops. She hurried out to him.

He was in one of the chairs, jiggling Chase on his knee, Chase smiling, gurgling.

Annie stopped and admired the scene. She didn't know why but she felt it was important to fix the sight in her memory. "Well, isn't this a pretty picture."

Thad looked up. "He's a great kid."

Annie nodded and took Chase from him. "He needs to sleep though, just like I do," she said, and she felt awkward about saying that last part. She didn't want to sleep now that Thad was there.

“Well.” Thad stood. “Like I said. I should go anyway.”

“No, I didn’t mean that.” She laid Chase on the bed. “And I was thinking, are you sure you can’t spend the night with us?” She walked over and pushed herself into him.

“It would be dangerous.”

She raised a shoulder. “But everything’s dangerous, Thad. And way out here we’re so far from the city. It’s like we’re in the middle of nowhere. What could be safer?”

He slid his hand under her chin, turned her face up to his and kissed her. He nodded.

“Good.” After holding each other for what seemed like forever, she said, “We really should sleep, though. I’ve got a plan B going with my friend Tara, and I’m going to need to be well-rested.”

“Plan B?”

“I’ll tell you in the morning.”

She set up Chase in the middle of the bed. “We’ll sleep on either side of him, okay?”

“Sure.” He kissed her.

She wanted more. She wanted so much more, but her feelings ran so deep for him that she knew—and he seemed to know too—that the physical stuff could wait.

They settled in the bed and shut the light. The room seemed so dark, so quiet, the only sound being Chase’s comfortable breathing as he slept. Careful not to wake him, Annie got up and walked to Thad’s side of the bed. “Move to the outside,” she whispered, pulling him toward the edge of the bed. She crawled in over him. Then with one arm holding Chase, she allowed herself to melt into Thad. She never knew when she fell asleep and whether she was dreaming, the feel and taste of Thad and his kiss lingering in her mind, body and soul.

* * *

Annie slept the whole night through. It was the first time Chase hadn't woken her. Was it possible he too sensed the stability and safety Thad brought to them? The rising sun was evident behind the drapes, the motel room's color being gradually restored as Annie lay in bed, feeling so good she didn't want to move a muscle. She knew problems would soon intrude and the reality of the situation would reassert itself, but for now she luxuriated in the peace.

A ring tone sounding so loud shattered the serenity. Annie looked at the little table where Thad's phone sat. "Don't answer it."

Thad rolled out of bed. "I have to. It's Eli's ring." He put the phone to his ear. He nodded a few times. "Got it."

Annie knew what was coming. "You have to go."

He nodded and stepped into his jeans. "Eli got a message from a friend of his. Delgado's got the make and model of my car. It won't be long till they pounce."

Annie exhaled deeply. "But I've so much to tell you. Plan B. All that."

He kissed her as he buttoned his shirt. He grabbed a pen from his laptop case and jotted on the motel stationary. "Here's my number. Buy a disposable cell and call, then toss it."

"Be safe, Thad."

He kissed her again and was gone.

She peeked out the window. Thad ran to a gray sedan, jumped in and sped out of the parking lot.

Annie was missing him already but she told herself to be strong for Chase's sake. They could still get this done. They still had to get this done.

Chase was rolling around, starting to cry. She checked—he needed to be changed. And he was probably hungry too. She looked outside again. Three police cruisers charged into the parking lot. She whisked the drapes shut. Chase was crying louder. “Yes, baby. I…” She’d almost said *Mommy*. “… will be right there.”

But the cops. Yes, Thad was gone but she and Chase weren’t. She tweaked the drapes again. Oh no. Two uniformed deputies were walking toward the door. There was no back exit. No fire escape. Only the pistol in the baby bag. But what, was she going to kill cops? Oh. She couldn’t think and Chase was crying really loud now. It was like a madness coming together: the timing seemed supernatural, even evil. A rap on the door.

Annie threw on the calypso pants. She wrapped Tara’s scarf tight on her head. More raps. Harder. Oh God. If they recognized her. Chase wailing, she picked him up, went to the door and called, “*Quien es?*”

She heard a groan from beyond the door.

*“Open up. Police. Policía. Abra la puerta.”*

Annie swallowed hard and, Chase still wailing, eased the door open. She shrugged, said, “*Si?*” and, keeping her head down, exaggeratedly paid attention to Chase’s crying.

A female deputy, sunglasses, long black hair with a center part, cruised by her into the room.

“*Que? Que paso?*” Annie said, doing her best to remember her Spanish class, and praying they wouldn’t recognize her.

The deputy at the door just nodded. Annie, meanwhile, hoped against hope the female deputy wouldn’t look in the baby bag or take the stationary with Thad’s number.

The woman came back shaking her head. Both deputies ignored Annie and stalked off. Annie shut the door and slumped against it. “Oh my,” she said. “I’m sorry,” she said to Chase, who finally was calming a little. She hurriedly changed him and gave him a bottle.

When the deputies cleared out of the parking lot so did she, heading straight for a Walmart to pick up a cheapie cell phone. She texted Tara: *we need to meet.*

# Chapter Twenty

Tara was working at the day camp but said she could take an early lunch, and Annie picked her up just outside Camp Lake Choctaw. Annie loaded Chase into the front pack baby sling, and she and Tara walked down residential side streets: neatly manicured lawns and rock gardens in front, cement block walls alley-side.

"Tara, is everything okay? The contest and all?"

Tara laughed. "Sure, Annie, everything's great. Oh yeah, there's the getting mobbed by all my friends looking for the inside track to the ten million, and oh, did I mention that now I'm getting death threats from Henry Buck, but besides that, yeah, things are great."

Annie hugged her friend. "I owe you so big-time for this."

"Yeah, you do," Tara said with a wink. She peeked at Chase. "How's the little guy doing?"

Annie smiled. "See for yourself." She turned the sling to her friend.

"Oh my God, Annie. He looks so much better than before. He looks…*happy*."

Annie glowed inside. But there was no time. "You sent the contest invites out?"

Tara nodded. "Annie, I had *twenty-five thousand* hits on my blog today. Terahawk Peak is going to be absolutely mobbed."

"What do people think it's going to be?"

"A mystery. I'm calling it *Campaign TBA*, 'to be announced,' and I even have a slogan: *Ten million is worth showing up for*."

"And people are going for that?"

"Yes. They know about the ten million from the media so

they know it's legit, and you give people a chance to win that much money, they're going to do all kinds of things."

"That is so awesome, Tara." A police cruiser rolled silently down the alley. Annie grabbed Tara's elbow and walked her the other way. "Cop."

"There's just one thing, Annie."

"What?"

"Your father stopped by to see me. He told me if I talk to you to tell you that he was wrong, and that he really wants to talk to you." Tara gazed down. "Annie, he seemed really pretty broken-up."

* * *

Annie thanked Tara and texted her father to meet her at a department store in Mesa. She picked the store because over the little valley the store was in stood a bluff from which she could see cars for miles around, and see if her father was being followed. She was angry at him, yes, but he was still her father and she still loved him.

She waited for his Volvo to roll into the lot. He was to park in the northeast corner, which he did. He got out of the car, walked around a while and eventually sat on the car's hood. Annie waited a full ten minutes to make sure he wasn't followed. To be extra sure, she gave Chase his bottle and waited some more. Finally, she drove the El Camino down.

She circled the lot's perimeter a few times before she pulled up to him. He jumped off the hood. She put the car in park and climbed out. "Hi, Dad."

He hugged her. "Honey, are you okay?"

She nodded.

"Honey, I want to tell you up front that I was wrong about

Monroe, and when you said he shot at you I nearly lost my mind." He bit his lip. "I fought with him in the SUV and came looking for you on the mountain when you got out of your car in that thunderstorm, but there was a flash flood, right in the gully you were in. Honey, I was afraid you might've even gotten caught in it."

"I did."

"Oh my God."

"Dad, there's no time to talk. I just wanted you to see I was okay."

"Honey, I'm working with a lawyer to help you. We're doing everything we can."

She nodded. "Gotta go." She turned back to the El Camino.

A slew of police cars rushed into the parking lot. Annie stared at her father.

"I didn't tell them. I didn't tell a soul. I swear."

She wasn't getting out of there by car. She wasn't getting out with Chase in her arms. She felt an excruciating pain in her heart, but she ran to the El Camino, pulled Chase from the car seat and handed him to her father. "Promise me you'll keep him safe."

"I will."

"Promise!"

"I promise."

She grabbed the pistol from the baby bag, stuffed it in her back pocket and ran for the department store. She could hear her father calling, "But what about you?"

People. Annie knew blending in with other people was her only chance. She forced herself to slow down when she got to the department store doors. In she went, breathing so hard but doing her best to hide it. She hurried to the women's section, her heart breaking because of giving up Chase, but she needed to be free to have any chance to ultimately save him, and her only chance of being free had been giving him up. She hurried to a counter topped by Styrofoam heads with wigs on them. She looked around, grabbed a blonde wig, dropped it on the floor, bent down for it, and when she came up she was a blonde. No time to switch clothes. Cops were spreading out across the store in a dragnet.

She headed for the back of the store, for the dressing rooms, bathrooms and loading docks. She took out the cheapie cell phone and the motel stationary with Thad's number. She dialed as she entered an employee area, probably a lunch room, poorly lit, tables littered with food wrappers, the walls lined with vending machines. A woman at one of the tables looked up. Annie nodded to her but kept walking. She stepped through a door into a warehouse area. Thad picked up on the second ring.

"I'm in trouble, Thad. I had to give up Chase. Cops are swarming me."

"Okay, Annie, now just keep your cool."

"It's just seconds till they get me. I'm at a department store—I can't even remember the name—on Hohokam and Westlake in Mesa. Can you pick me up?"

"Yes."

"There's a bluff over the store to the east. Do you know it?"

"No."

"Well, you can't miss it. When you get near the store's entrance take Frontage Road. It heads up toward the bluff, then once you get near the bluff, you'll have to go off-road to get to the very top."

"Give me twenty minutes."

"I'll be there." She hung up. "I hope," she said under her

breath. Two workers were talking at a conveyor belt. They gawked at her as she approached.

"Well, hello," one of them said, his eyes widening, his denim shirt sweaty and grimy.

Annie stopped. She smiled. She smelled smoke. "Hi, guys. I got a little turned around. I was looking for the back exit."

The other man comfortably took a drag off a cigarette. He nodded behind Annie. "The store's back in there."

"Yes, thanks." The cops would be on her in seconds. "That's the thing," she said, "I'm not a customer. I'm corporate."

The men laughed.

Annie realized how ridiculous she must look in her calypso pants, high-tops and the wig, but she put on her most serious face and an even more serious air. She extended her hand. "Elaine Richardson, corporate VP in HR."

The smoker dropped his cigarette and stomped on it. He wiped his hand on his pants before shaking. "Mike Cardi. Shipping and Receiving."

His co-worker tucked in his shirt and put out his hand. "Joe Olesiak. The same."

"Good to meet you two." Annie smiled. "Now that rear exit?"

They jumped to the side. Cardi pointed to a five-step staircase. "You just walk up those steps, down the landing to that little door on the left and that takes you right out onto the dock."

"Men." Annie nodded. She took off for the staircase.

It was as the man had said. The little door led to a three-bay loading dock, with only one truck docked. She sat on the dock, then jumped down to the pavement. To the west led downhill to the parking lot—and Delgado and his deputies. To the east was the bluff, steep and probably loaded with rattlesnakes. Annie ran toward the parking lot, at least fifty yards from the docks, and threw her wig next to the building. Then she ran to the bluff.

This was one time she was glad she was wearing the high-tops. If she'd had heels she couldn't have even attempted the climb. As it was, it was going to be hard enough.

An enormous dead tree, gray and twisted, was at the base of the bluff, scrawny green bushes and sagebrush farther up and all the way up to the top were red rocks, most small but some huge, boulders really. Annie kept running—the base of the bluff was the easy part—but soon the increased slope slowed her to a fast walk. She turned to look at the dock. Nobody yet. She continued up, the slope even steeper now, her face just a couple feet from the red rocks as she climbed. She turned to look again. She blew out a deep breath. She was quite a ways up already—it would be a long fall if she lost her footing. Still no cops. Wait! Four of Delgado's deputies rushed out onto the dock. Annie scrambled behind a bush.

Two of the deputies headed west toward the parking lot, while the other two walked at the bluff. Annie settled behind the bush, thorny branches grazing her face. The bush was not that thick, and all she could do was hope she was fully hidden. Hope and pray. She thought of Eli's Great Spirit. She shook her head. If there were such a thing, the Great Spirit had gotten her into this mess in the first place—why should she pray to something that would do that?

The two deputies lingered at the base of the bluff, probably thinking no one in their right mind would attempt to scale something so steep. Then Annie heard it. A rattle. The deputies were scanning the bluff. If she moved, they'd spot her. More rattling. She saw a snake, black and silver, slithering along the bush's branches with evil fluidity, flicking its tongue. She remembered what Eli had said about the rattler checking her out after the flash flood. It had thought she was probably too big to eat. Not the most comforting thought, but at least it was something. The snake headed for her. For her face. She closed her eyes. Only seeing Chase in her mind's eye. Her desire to save him. Her *love* for him. Kept her there.

Then she heard a yell. She opened her eyes—the snake inches from her face, flicking, poised for a strike—and saw the two deputies that had been scanning the bluff running toward the deputy who'd yelled. The deputy was waving the blonde wig.

Annie eased away from the bush, tripped over a rock and fell backward. "Oh," she cried, but she was so grateful to be away from the snake. She turned to check on the deputies. All four had taken off for the parking lot.

It took everything she had but she worked her way to the top of the bluff.

No Thad.

She called him.

"Annie, they set up a roadblock. I had to come off-road from the south. I'm just reaching the top of the bluff now."

She turned and an emerald green Lexus SUV with tinted windows came flying up onto the bluff. She ran toward it.

The passenger door swung open and she jumped in.

"Annie, you okay?" Thad was wearing a blue cap with a red W on it.

"Yeah."

"Got the cell?"

"Yeah."

"Give it to me."

She handed it over. “And I’ve still got my phone.”

“Give me that too.”

She did.

He jumped out and whipped the phones as far as he could down the bluff. He jumped back in and punched the gas pedal. “What all just happened here?”

Annie felt a deep sadness in her gut. It was hitting her—she’d given Chase away.

“Annie?”

She turned to him. “What?”

He looked at her. “What’s wrong?”

She sighed. “I told you—I had to give up Chase.”

He nodded. He was headed along the bluff to the north, much slower now, the SUV rolling over fallen logs, mounds, boulders. It was like being in a washing machine. “But what brought you out here in the first place?”

“I was meeting my father.”

“You were *what?*”

It sounded like an accusation. “I was meeting my father, Thad. It’s just something I felt I had to do.”

“But didn’t you realize he’d be tailed?” He slowed to go over a particularly big boulder, the SUV dropping down after it cleared.

“Well, I guess I made a mistake, but if you don’t mind, I don’t need to feel any worse than I already do.”

“Yeah. Okay. I hear you.” He reached over and squeezed her shoulder.

Oh, his touch felt so good. But especially now she needed to keep thinking about Chase. “Thad,” she said softly. “I have to get to the top of Stony Peak tomorrow by noon. It’ll be my last chance to save Chase. Will you help me?"

"Of course, I'll help you," Thad said, finally stopping farther along the bluff, where he came to a paved road. "But right now, tonight, you're going to have the whole world after you."

Annie remembered Tara's text: *Annie whole frickin world is after u.* "And now they'll have a pretty good idea what I look like, even with the black hair."

"They had a pretty good idea before, Annie. Now they'll know exactly."

"How so?"

Thad shrugged. "Most likely a drone."

"Like in Iraq and Afghanistan?"

"No. More like a surveillance drone. They have cameras with zoom lenses that can read the date on a penny on the ground."

"Great." She rolled her eyes. "Well, let me ask you this then —is there *any* good news?"

He looked at her and smiled. "We're together."

Well, that much was true. Annie smiled back. "Now we have to help Chase, though. I gave him to my father. He promised to take care of him but you know how relentless Monroe is."

"There are always options, Annie."

He'd spoken so calmly and authoritatively. "Thad, tell me the truth, you're more than a newspaper reporter, aren't you?"

He wheeled the SUV around and in the distance they could see the department store parking lot. Police cruisers, their lights flashing, TV news vans, their antennas stretching high, reporters, cameramen hustling about. "Annie, take a look. Right now we've got more important things to deal with."

He was right of course, but she still wanted to know. And she wanted the truth and the intimacy of him sharing it with her. "So you're not going to tell me?"

He sighed. "I'll give you the *Reader's Digest* version. I'm not and I am."

"You're not more than a newspaper reporter and you are?"

"Exactly." He threw the SUV into park. "Now you said you came up Frontage. I could head back there, but do you think there's any chance of getting out that way?"

He was putting her off but what could she do. "No."

He peered in the other direction. "And this way is going to take us straight out into the desert."

"There's no way we're getting out on Frontage, Thad."

# Chapter Twenty-one

They headed into the desert. Annie knew this was the real Arizona desert, no longer tamed by man-made development. Her father had explained it to her. The Arizona desert was wild, unforgiving. Then when development arrived, golf courses were put in, canals, all kinds of things that moderated the harsh conditions. But the real Arizona desert was still there, just a little farther out. They drove for an hour, the Lexus running great, comfortable with the air conditioning. But the terrain was getting more and more rugged. Rugged even for a four wheel drive vehicle like the Lexus. The sun would be going down soon and Annie was getting a little concerned—and getting more than a little excited to be alone in the middle of nowhere with Thad. “We’re getting pretty far out,” she said.

He braked to a halt. A tall spindly cactus was to their left. In the distance were the mountains, dimming in the fading sunlight. “Yeah.”

“So what are we going to do?”

He rubbed his chin, a five-o’clock shadow rising. “Well, there’s not enough light to make it back the way we came. The headlights simply won’t cut it as dark as it gets out here.”

“So, what?” It already looked pitch black out the side tinted windows. “Remember I need to get to Stony Peak by tomorrow at noon.”

“Tomorrow won’t be a problem but right now it’s like I said, the whole world is after you. Roadblocks will be set up. I really think that for right now, here is just about the safest place we can be.”

Spending the night alone in the desert with Thad. She sighed inwardly. It was a most pleasant proposition. And with all this craziness with Monroe—he'd shot at her for God's sake—and Delgado, Annie felt like she didn't really know how long either of them had to live. If somebody had proposed this situation to her a week ago, she would have said absolutely no way. But as it was…

Thad looked at her and grinned. "So what do you think?"

…as it was, maybe it wasn't such a bad idea. She'd told him she loved him. It had been a fiery passionate moment but she did love him. "I think it might not be such a bad idea."

"I've got a gallon of water and a survival kit in back. We'll be okay. And…" Was he blushing? "…when I put the back seats down there'll be plenty of room for us to stretch out."

She leaned over and hugged him. "So will this be like the last good night on the *Titanic?*"

"Nah," he said and smiled. "You gotta think positive. Things have a way of working out when you do the right thing."

She laughed. "Now you're starting to sound like Eli."

He nodded. "Eli knows a lot."

"I suppose."

He killed the engine. "Might as well save the gas, make sure we have enough to get back."

Annie opened her window.

"Ah," he said. "That's probably okay for a while but I wouldn't keep it open long."

"Why not?"

"Well, snakes."

"They're going to come through the window?"

"They're crafty, Annie. And out here there's a lot of them. There's a lot more of everything out here. It's not like in town, or on hiking trails. It’s really wild.”

She buzzed the window up. “Anything else I should be worried about?”

“Me maybe.” He smiled.

She gazed at him. She loved his face, the world-weariness of it somehow, the bags under his eyes, his olive skin. “Okay. So we stay here. What are we going to do all night?”

He shrugged. “We could always make out.”

She laughed. “So *that’s* why you drove me all the way out here.”

“Yeah, that’s it,” he said with a wink, and he slid his hand along the back of her neck and with a twinkle in his eye said, “Hey, you know I never got a chance to compliment you on your outfit choice. Very stylish.”

“Ha!” She looked down at her plaid top, the calypso pants, the high-tops. “Your buddy Eli gave me these after I got caught in a flash flood. And I felt like such an idiot, pretending to be a corporate executive back at the department store. Oh my God.”

“You thirsty?”

“Not really.”

“Hungry? I’ve got energy bars in the emergency kit.”

She shook her head.

He nodded toward the back. “Come on then. I want to hold you.”

*That* sounded good. That sounded really good. She nodded.

* * *

Annie’s heart fluttered as Thad set up the back of the Lexus. He was saying how he’d camped out in it before and slept as comfortable as if he’d been in his own bed. She asked him if he’d made it in the morning. He laughed. It was such sweet anticipation Annie hardly wanted it to end. She marveled remembering that it hadn't been that long ago when she thought he might be dead, shot by Sheriff Delgado in that high school parking lot. Then he'd been in jail. One way or another she'd thought she might never see him again, and here she was going to have him all to herself all night. Oh, it was time. He was beckoning her back.

The sun slipped below the horizon and darkness fell quickly. Annie crawled over the slight rise of the bent-down backseat. "Here I come."

He was waiting with open arms.

Oh God, she thought as those arms enfolded her. This felt so right, so real, so *good*, and it was so different from the drama she'd been living through lately it almost overwhelmed her. It was as if she could feel herself coming back to life, the life of who she really was. She didn't realize she was crying quietly—from joy—until Thad spoke.

"Hey. You okay?"

She nodded into his chest. "I'm just happy."

He pulled her even closer.

So tightly held. So safe. So comfortable. So loved. But also so exhausted—she fell asleep. She awoke to the sound of animals yelping and crying fiercely. It was so pitch black it took a few moments to orient herself, but she recognized Thad by smell, and then little by little things started falling into place. "What's that noise?"

"Just some coyotes," he said, stroking her cheek, her hair.

"Are they dangerous?"

"To rabbits and mice. They just smell us and their hunger is making them crazy."

"How many are there?"

He shrugged. "It's a pack. Probably twenty or thirty."

"Oh my God."

"Relax, Annie. They can't hurt us."

"They're just so creepy-sounding, yipping and howling like that."

"Like I said, it's wild out here."

"I've seen coyotes in town before, on golf courses and near canals, but they've always been alone, and I've never heard them."

"There's a lot more of them out here."

"I guess I knew that but even so, it's startling. It's dangerous."

"Coyotes aren't the only dangerous things out here. There's bobcats, and although I've never seen one, mountain lions."

"Well." She snuggled into him. "I'm not going to worry about it."

The yelping of the coyotes died down. Annie could hear Thad's breath. Then she heard a rattle and felt a sharp pain in her ankle. "Thad!"

"Annie, don't move."

"Something bit me!"

"Don't move. I mean it—don't move." He flicked on a flashlight. Coiled in the corner of the SUV sat a brown rattlesnake, its rattler sticking up at a ninety degree angle, rattling.

"Oh God, Thad, my ankle hurts. And it's a rattlesnake."

Thad frowned. "A Mojave Rattler."

"Oh God."

"Annie, listen to me. First bites by rattlesnakes more often than not have very little venom. They're just warnings. Now just don't move."

He pulled a reflector from the emergency kit and slowly crawled toward the snake. "Easy, boy, easy." The snake flicked its tongue, its rattler churning furiously. "Easy." He held the reflector out in his left hand and gradually brought it nearer the snake. The snake struck the reflector with lightning speed. When it recoiled, Thad grabbed it by the neck. The snake reeled, twisted and writhed but Thad had it securely. He raised the hatchback. With a sudden, decisive move he pitched the snake into the darkness and slammed the hatch.

"Thad, my leg is bleeding."

"That's normal."

"But what are we going to do? We're so far away from everything."

He looked her in the eye. "Annie, listen to me. I'm going to tell it to you straight. That snake *was* a rattlesnake but chances are it did not inject a large amount of venom. We still need to get you to an emergency room but the most important thing you can do right now is stay calm. If you don't, the venom, the toxins, will spread faster and farther into your system. So I know you're upset but you need to do the best you can to stay calm."

Annie inhaled deeply. "Okay."

Thad scrambled into the driver's seat and started the engine.

"Turn the inside light on."

He did.

"It's still bleeding."

"That's okay. That's normal. Annie, I'm going to shut the light."

She closed her eyes and sighed. "Go ahead."

Back in darkness she was thinking maybe another snake had

gotten in. Her heart raced. But Thad had said to stay calm. Stay calm. She lay back. The odds of there being another snake were extremely small. No, she would help herself by staying calm. But how to keep the negative thoughts away? It was difficult. Bit by a rattlesnake in the middle of nowhere.

She told herself to get a grip. Yes, she'd been bitten by a rattlesnake—the SUV dropped down after rocking over a boulder—but she was being driven to the hospital to get help. Okay, she could handle. And she couldn't forget about Chase.

But the pain was shooting up her leg and she was starting to feel weird. Not quite nauseous, just weird. Light-headed maybe. "Thad, I feel strange. Like I might faint."

"Just hang, Annie. We'll be at the hospital soon."

Soon. Hang. Stay calm. She felt a tingling in her lips, then her face, hands, the other foot. "John, my face, my hands, both feet are tingling." Oh my God, had she called Thad by the wrong name? Was her mind going?

"We're almost to the gravel road. Remember what I told you—stay calm."

Stay calm. Stay calm. Stay calm. But the pain was getting worse. And what about Chase? Stony Peak? The contest at noon? "What time is it?"

"Quarter past four."

The SUV lurched violently, then dropped to the earth.

Thad smacked the steering wheel. "Damn it!"

"Thad." She looked at him, his face just barely visible in the reflected light of the dash.

He clenched his jaw. "We're almost to the road but—"

"But?"

"We're almost to the road, but we're going to have to walk

the last mile or so."

"Why?"

"The front axle just broke going over a boulder."

"But I don't know if I *can* walk."

"Don't worry about it."

"But—"

He turned to her. "Annie." He flipped on the map light and made sure he had her eye. "Do you trust me?"

"Yes." She did. "But the coyotes?"

"We've got the pistol."

"Thad." Now she had his eye. "Are we really going to be okay?"

He nodded, then opened his door. In seconds he was around back, lifting the hatch. "Can you scoot toward me?"

She pushed herself forward with her arms. "Is this far enough?"

"It's great. Now you've got the pistol?"

"In my pocket."

"Okay." He leaned in and lifted her out, she twining her arms around his neck. He held her with one arm and shut the hatch. "Okay, here we go." They started across the mountain.

All Annie could see was sky and stars and the outline of Thad's face. He was breathing hard, taking guarded steps, testing steps in the darkness. "Are you okay?" she asked. "I'm not too heavy?"

Coyotes yelped in the distance.

"I'm fine." Anticipating her concern he said, "They're far off. They won't be a problem."

She clutched him tighter. Stay calm. Stay calm.

# Chapter Twenty-two

"Where am I?" Annie said, looking around the empty room. It was obviously a hospital room, the green curtains—nylon mesh atop, on trolleys—the IV stand, beeping, the tube running into the back of her hand. Disoriented, she might as well have asked herself, *Who* am I?

Give yourself time, she told herself. Coughing came from the stall next to hers. The pain in her leg was better but she still felt weird, muddled. Where was Thad? What about the police? She checked to make sure she wasn't handcuffed. And what about Stony Peak? The contest? Noon? What time was it?

She shifted, inadvertently pulling on the IV, and a louder beeping sounded. After a minute, a nurse in purple scrubs zinged the curtain open. She smiled. "Well, hello. Welcome back." She pushed a switch on the IV monitor and the louder beeping stopped. "Have a nice sleep?"

"Still a little woozy."

"That's not surprising. The combination of snake venom and pain meds make for quite a potent cocktail. How's the pain?"

"It's getting better…but…" Should she ask about Thad? Where was he? "…I came with…"

The nurse nodded, her blonde bangs falling across her eyes. "Jimmy will be right back. He said he had to run a quick errand."

Jimmy? Okay. Jimmy. Thad used an alias. "Thanks."

"Sure thing. Listen, I'm your nurse and my name is Lisa. I'm on till three this afternoon. If—"

"What time is it now?"

"A clock's behind you on the wall." She nodded. "It's ten-thirty-nine in the morning."

"Oh my God!"

"What's wrong, Ellen?"

Annie took *Ellen* in stride. Thad was Jimmy and she was Ellen. "Oh, nothing. I'm just surprised I was out so long."

"It's good you were. It gave your body time to recover. You were lucky Jimmy got you in here as fast as he did."

Annie nodded.

"Anyway." The nurse picked up the call button. "I'm sure you know what this is. Just press it if you need anything."

The nurse left. Ten-thirty-nine! No Thad! She had to be at Stony Peak at noon! If she didn't show, people would figure it was a hoax and her last chance to save Chase would be gone.

The curtain tweaked open. Thad peered in. "Are you decent, Ellen?"

She laughed, her head hurting a little. "Yes, Jimmy."

He slid in between the curtains. "How you feeling?"

"I'm okay. Still a little woozy. How are you?"

"I'm good but I'm not going to be able to hang around. I was just listening in on a police radio. Sheriff Delgado's men found the Lexus and the blood in the back. They're going to put two and two together. Chances are they'll be here in a flash."

"And what about me, Thad? *I'm* going to hang around? I've got to be at Stony Peak at noon or all hope of saving Chase is lost."

"You need the medical attention." He crossed his arms. "It's over, Annie. You did your best."

"No, Thad, I don't accept that. I'm getting up." She leaned forward, strained the IV, the louder beeping sounding again.

The nurse returned. "Ah, I see Jimmy's back." She nodded to

him. “Now what are you doing to this IV, young lady?” she said with a smile and switched off the beeping.

“So, Lisa,” Thad said, “when is Ellen going to be able to get out of here?”

The nurse grabbed a chart hanging on a hook at the foot of the bed. “That will be up to the doctor and he doesn’t do rounds till noon, but he already told me he wants to keep her at least one night for observation. You were right. It was Mojave rattler venom and that is the really nasty stuff.” She left.

“You heard her.” Thad walked to Annie’s side and brushed his hand across her forehead. “You’re lucky to be alive.”

She pushed his hand aside. “I’m not letting Chase down, Thad. I’m getting out of here one way or another. Now are you going to help me or not?”

He smiled. “Why did I have a feeling you were going to say that.”

“Well?”

He walked to a little blue chest of drawers and opened one of them. He pulled out an alcohol packet and a bandage. “You ready?”

“We’re just going to walk out?”

“If you can. If not, I’ll carry you.”

“And they won’t say anything?”

“Oh, they might. If they see us.”

“And if they do?”

“Then we just keep walking. Annie, it’s a hospital, not a prison. They can’t keep you here against your will.”

“Huh.” She looked at him and then nodded toward the IV in her hand.

He eased out the tube, wiped the tiny spot of blood, applied the bandage, and they walked out of the hospital.

* * *

They walked out of the hospital to a black all-terrain Hummer SUV. Annie felt like she was getting into a tank and she laughed. She looked at Thad who piled in and fired the engine. She knew he'd stolen it. "And just where did you get this from?"

"Uh." He drove off, leaving a little of the tires' rubber on the hospital lot. "It was a friend of a friend's."

Oh well. It was for a good cause, she figured. She filled him in on just what the contest at Stony Peak was going to be, that the people coming for the ten million would actually be at Terahawk Peak, but that she was going to make her pitch from the adjacent Stony Peak with a bullhorn. He said he knew of a place that would have the gear she needed. They headed for the highway.

She was woozy but she still wanted to know just what his real story was. "You know, Thad, I keep asking about who you really are and you keep putting me off. Is there any chance of you telling me now?"

He sighed. "Annie, did you ever think that maybe what I'm not telling you, I don't want to tell myself?"

She could see that he was hurting. "So are you saying you weren't really in Afghanistan and Iraq?"

He frowned, then said, "Oh, I was there all right."

She waited.

"I just wasn't an aid worker."

Annie swallowed. "So what were you?"

He cleared his throat. "Uh."

She looked at his face. It was a face that cared. Deeply. But now it was in anguish. "Thad."

"Cove Ops."

"Cove what?"

"I was in special forces in Covert Military Operations."

Annie had heard the term but that was about it. "So you were in the army?"

"I worked for the government. Annie, I did some bad things over there."

Bad things. She didn't want to but knew she had to know what he was talking about. "Bad things?"

"Annie, we were a covert op. No oversight. We did night raids, okay? We had kill lists."

"But the people on the lists were the bad guys, right? Our enemies. You were defending us."

He shook his head. "That's what I thought when I signed on, but that's not the way it worked all the time."

She started to say something but he spoke before she could get the words out.

"I shot and killed a pregnant woman."

Annie felt tears well behind her eyes. She sank down in her seat.

Thad's chin was quivering. "It was a night raid. A known target, a high-ranking Taliban, was confirmed in the house. Things just happened too fast. People were yelling. All kinds of movement. We couldn't secure it. Someone jumped from behind a door. I pulled my trigger."

They rode along in silence.

"That's when I knew I had to get out. And that's when I met Eli too, and he felt the same way. We both wanted to get out and do something good with our lives. To make up for—" His voice broke. "—for what we did."

"So you and Eli were in the army together?"

"Special forces. Eli was one of the helicopter pilots who flew us in for the night raids."

It was a lot to take in, so much so that Annie, her head still woozy, had practically forgotten about what she had to do and where she was going. But the bold sheer face of Superstition Mountain was coming into view reminding her as they barreled down the highway, the Hummer's heavily treaded tires screaming against the pavement. She'd have to sort out later how she felt about what Thad had told her because right now it had to be all about helping Chase.

* * *

Annie was still light-headed from the snake venom and pain meds, but even so, she was able to at least somewhat grasp what Thad was briefing her on about the gear she would need as they pulled up to a warehouse on the outskirts of Apache Junction.

On the outside, the warehouse was shabby, worn-down, looked abandoned even. Inside, it was spotless, polished concrete floors, a faint chemical smell in the air. Thad, holding her elbow to steady her, led Annie to a corner of the warehouse where he opened a huge locker filled with electronic equipment. He removed a cardboard box from the locker.

He took a foot-long wire from the box and stretched it out. "Now this mic is going to transmit live *and* record everything on a digital memory card." At one end of the wire was a tiny microphone, on the other end a card the size of a fingernail. "Everything you say and anything anyone around you says is going to be recorded on this."

"But *you'll* hear me?"

"Every word, Annie. Every breath." He fitted her with the wire.

She removed a red and white bullhorn from the locker. "I'll need this but will it be loud enough? Will the sound carry? I mean, the peaks aren't that close."

"That bullhorn has fifty watts of power. The sound will easily carry over a mile."

Annie was starting to feel like *she* was in the special forces, or whatever Thad had called it, but she was definitely glad to have him helping her. Now they'd have to hustle to get to Stony Peak in time. "Let's go."

"You're comfortable with how to use everything?"

There wasn't much to do. Pull the trigger on the bullhorn. She figured he was really asking if she was coherent—and she wasn't sure she was. "No problem."

"And you'll take the pistol?"

"No." She shook her head. "I'm not. It'll be what it'll be but I'm not shooting anybody."

"Well, if things go as I expect, you shouldn't have to, but if you don't want it, don't take it."

"I don't want it."

"Okay, then here we go."

They went out to the Hummer, Annie shaking off Thad's help this time. She stepped up onto the running board and climbed in. She watched as Thad loaded the bullhorn and a long canvas bag onto the back seat. Her right eye was twitching and she wasn't sure if it was from the snake bite, the pain meds or the fear racing through her body like a flash fire. But she would do what she had to do, because this wasn't about her any more. It was about Chase and she wasn't going to let him down.

They headed for Stony Peak.

"You sure you're okay?"

Annie wiped the sweat from her forehead. "I'm fine." She thought of Stony Peak and how her father had never taken her there because of all the loose stones and boulders and how difficult it would be to get up it. "Are you sure this thing can climb Stony Peak?"

Thad just smiled. "There's only one road up to the peak. Once I drop you there, I'm going to drag, with the Hummer's help, a huge boulder to block the road. When it's all said and done, I'll move the boulder and come get you."

"Can't you stay with me at the top?"

He shook his head. "I'll be more benefit to you lower where I can keep an eye on things, keep my finger on the pulse of what's happening."

Traffic on the highway was heavy. When they exited on Ironwood Drive it was crawling. Thad drove on the shoulder. "Looks like your friend's campaign is hugely working."

"Yes."

A half mile from the peaks, traffic came to a standstill and Thad had to drive into the desert to get to the road for Stony Peak. "Now," he said, looking over when he got there, "this is going to be a pretty steep incline."

"Okay," Annie said but when the Hummer went nearly vertical she felt so woozy she nearly passed out. Oh, the pressure was squeezing her brain. She'd never had much occasion to pray in her life before but… She thought of Eli's Great Spirit. "Just help me get through this, G.S.," she said under her breath.

"What was that?"

She shook her head. "Nothing."

Stones and small boulders were strewn across the road, evidence of the instability of the terrain and frequent rock slides.

They were going up the back side of the peak.

"So," Annie said, "we won't see anything till we reach the very top?"

A quick nod from Thad. The Hummer's tires were slipping on the loose stones, then re-gripping.

Chase, Annie thought. She just kept thinking about Chase. This was all for him. The Hummer was finally on the verge of cresting the peak when it stopped. "Why'd you stop here? Won't it make the next few feet?"

"It'll make it but it'll be better if they don't see a vehicle. If you think you're able, you should climb the next few feet on your own."

She could do it for Chase. She took a deep breath and opened her door.

"Wait." Thad reached into the back seat and gave her the bullhorn. "And one more thing." He pulled her to him and kissed her. "See you in a little bit."

Annie nodded and climbed out of the Hummer.

# Chapter Twenty-three

Annie could feel the energy, the electricity charging the atmosphere as she climbed the last few feet to the top of Stony Peak. The noonday sun was powering down. The air still. A murmuring rising. A few more feet. She walked around a big cactus and she was at the top.

"Oh my." Every inch of Terahawk Peak was filled with people. Thousands of them. The mountain a sea of colors. Some people sat in deck chairs. Others stood. Many held umbrellas. A beach ball bounced from one stalk of quickly extending arms to another. The taller cacti were all that protruded from the human carpet and every boulder was occupied as a prized perch. Annie thought, wouldn't it be nice if she could just let things stay this way? Maybe she could join them. Just blend in. A bead of sweat ran down her back.

Yes, it seemed to be a carnival atmosphere, but she knew it wasn't. These people thought she was an evil baby stealer. These people wanted to collect ten million dollars by handing her over to Monroe—dead or alive. She turned to look for Thad but he was gone.

She raised the bullhorn to her lips but didn't pull the trigger on the handle. No one saw her. Or if they did she couldn't tell. The crowd just kept doing its thing but she sensed a tension rising in it too. It had to be a hundred and fifteen in the shade, a hundred and thirty in the sun. She pulled the trigger.

"I want to thank you all for coming." She lowered the bullhorn and looked again at the crowd. She couldn't tell if they'd heard. But they must've because the bullhorn was so loud and

Thad said its sound carried for a mile. She raised it back up.

"My name is Annie Rebarchek and I know you're all here because of me." She pulled the bullhorn down and looked again. She still couldn't tell if they were hearing. She raised it. "Ten million dollars is a lot of money. I know Houston Monroe's offering it makes him look like a hero, but I am here to tell you that Houston Monroe is no hero."

Finally there was movement in the crowd, the fringes bleeding away from the whole and heading for Stony Peak—to get her. No time to waste. Up went the bullhorn. "Houston Monroe had neglected and abused baby Chase to the point where he nearly died." The crowd was clearly moving now, like a mass of jelly slowly rolling into the valley separating the two peaks. "Monroe would like to do away with all human beings that don't measure up to his warped standard of perfection and is conducting eugenics experiments in pursuit of a Nazi-like utopian vision. Baby Chase was one of those heartless experiments." The leading edge of people were at the base of Stony Peak now. It was slow going ascending, but like mountain goats they hobbled over stones and boulders, a surge of humanity rising—to get her.

Shots fired behind. She whirled but couldn't see anything. Were they shooting at Thad? Was Thad shooting at them? Was someone shooting at her? She turned back and when she did she saw a boulder, dislodged by one of the climbers, tumbling down the mountain, many diving out of the way in time, some not so lucky. But the tide of humanity continued its steady rise—to get her.

Up went the bullhorn. "Houston Monroe has bought off Sheriff Delgado and intimidated the media. I am not the evil baby stealer they have made me out to be. I'm a seventeen-year-old high school junior at Alameda High in the valley, and all I did was rescue poor baby Chase who was being so abused. All I did was save him from being *killed* by Monroe."

She felt a rush of wind in her ear and realized a rock had just whizzed by her head. She put the bullhorn down. The first line of climbers, mostly twenty-something guys, was nearly at the top. She whipped up the bullhorn. "All I ask is that you investigate what I'm saying for yourselves. I ask you for Chase's sake!" She dropped the bullhorn. The first line of climbers crawled over the crest. "Thad, come get me!"

More shots were fired and she ran to the road and saw Thad standing on the Hummer's roof firing a rifle into the air, while a crowd swelled greedily, encroachingly on the road below him. She turned back. A guy in a red dago-T, biceps bulging, hurled a rock at her. She heard more shots.

And more shots, but the sound of the shots was turning into a thudding noise, and then a sharp breeze hit her. She looked up. A helicopter dangling a rope ladder was descending. She covered her eyes from the blast of wind and sun's glare but thought *it must be Eli!* She glanced at the mob charging her. The bottom rung of the ladder was within reach. She looked for Thad. Then back at the mob. She grabbed the ladder and started climbing.

The helicopter rose. Annie looked up for Eli but the wind from the chopper blades blurred her eyes. She looked down at the mob. They were still throwing rocks but the rocks fell well short of her—she must be rising quickly. She checked for Thad. The Hummer was driving around the boulder blocking Stony Peak's road. She looked up again for Eli but still the wind blurred her eyes. When she looked back down she got a *whoosh* of vertigo. Oh, she was suddenly so high, so quickly. The rock throwers were ants. Thad's Hummer a matchbox. She kept climbing the ladder.

Step by step she rose. She quit looking up because with each step the rush of wind from the chopper blades intensified. She forced herself one handhold, one foothold, one rung up at a time. At last the helicopter's landing skids were within reach. A sliding door opened. She was almost there. Almost. With every last bit of strength she climbed in.

She rolled onto the helicopter floor and looked up to see Houston Monroe.

* * *

"Welcome to Green Magic One, Annie." Monroe smiled derisively. "I must admit you've had quite a run but your luck just ran out."

Annie sucked in a quick breath. The helicopter door slid shut behind her. "You're the one who's out of luck, Monroe. All those people down there just heard how you've abused Chase," she said, hoping it was true.

Monroe—all in white, a headset over his perfectly coiffed hair, designer sunglasses—laughed. "Okay. If you say so."

Annie nodded but she also remembered how sending the photos of the abused Chase to reporters hadn't changed a thing. How nothing she'd done had changed a thing. Monroe seemed to win at every turn. But she wasn't giving in. She'd never give in. She pulled herself up to a sitting position. "They heard, Monroe. They heard."

He smiled. "I suppose you'll be okay in prison. You're pretty resilient. What do you think?"

"I think you're disturbed."

"Well…" he said, banking the chopper sharply, Annie grabbing onto one of the seat posts to keep from sliding across the floor. "…fortunately what you think makes absolutely no difference whatsoever."

She bit her lip. "So why did you save me? That mob down there would've torn me limb from limb."

"Oh my goodness," he said with a head shake. "You're really not very bright, are you? I can give you *ten million* reasons why I saved you. Not to mention the public relations disaster you getting torn to pieces by a mob would've caused me."

Annie shook her head. And she'd thought it would be Eli. She laughed. Eli and his Great Spirit. Where was his Great Spirit now? Then it hit her—she was wearing the microphone that Thad said would record everything she said *and* everything anyone nearby said. She wondered if she was close enough for it to pick up Monroe.

"Monroe, can I at least sit in the co-pilot's chair, put on a seat belt?"

Monroe was silent for a minute. Then he shrugged. "Why not. In fact I think it might be an excellent idea for the media to photograph you safely strapped in when we land."

Annie climbed onto the seat and buckled herself in.

"Ever flown in a helicopter before?"

"No."

"Well, this isn't just any helicopter. It's a Sikorsky S-92, one of the fastest helicopters in the world."

"So you can get me to jail in a hurry?"

Monroe laughed mirthlessly. "That's one way of looking at it."

"You know, Monroe, since you're going to have me thrown into prison maybe you could at least answer a few questions."

"Oh, I don't think so."

Annie figured she had nothing to lose. "It's funny but I always saw you as such a giving sort of person, such a positive influence on society. Environmentalism. Wiping out the brown cloud. I don't know. From my way of looking at it, you doing the eugenics experiments just didn't seem to fit."

He looked at her with a wry smile.

"Everything with you was always so positive positive positive. You seemed like you genuinely wanted to help people. That's why with the eugenics I never understood why—"

"Why?" He glared at her. "All right, let me ask you a question then. How do you think this gorgeous, sleek, top-performing helicopter came to be?"

Annie shrugged.

"It didn't just appear. It didn't hatch out of an egg. It didn't fall out of the sky ready-made. No. It was made by improving on previous models. Improving is everything. Improving moves the world forward."

"So your eugenics experiments are improving humans?"

"Exactly."

"And the fact that what you were doing was killing Chase didn't matter?"

"You know nothing about Chase."

"Then tell me about him."

Monroe rolled his neck and exhaled deeply. "Chase has been an experiment from the very start. He's not even naturally human. He was made in a lab, designed, created to be an experiment. If something bad happens to him, it's simply the cost of R&D."

"R&D?"

"Research and Development. Improving."

"So you'd let an innocent little baby die?"

"To move the entire human race forward, you bet I would. No doubt about it. And let me tell you something, Chase wouldn't be the first baby who died serving the cause of universal progress, and he won't be the last."

Hearing that, Annie felt like throwing up. "That's sick, Monroe." But now she had his own words incriminating him on the memory disk of the wireless she wore. And Thad hopefully heard all of it too. Now if she could just somehow get Thad the disk. But Monroe was flying her to the sheriff, to jail. She'd be searched. Oh God. "What would you say if I told you I had all of what you just said recorded on a memory disk?"

"I would say you've been reading too many spy novels. But just in case…" He raised an eyebrow. "…now that you mention it, I'll make sure Delgado's deputies strip search you when we land." He laughed.

A green flash shot across the helicopter.

"What the hell!" Monroe yelled.

Annie clutched her sides.

Monroe's head swiveled like it was on a stick, searching all around. He reached for a switch on the instrument panel. "This is Sikorsky S-92. Are there any other aircraft in the area? I just experienced what I think was a near-miss."

Annie snugged her seat belt.

A swirling shark-like camouflage-green helicopter swooped in front of them, then veered straight up, disappearing from view.

"Damn it! That's a AH-64D Apache Long Bow, an army attack helicopter!" Monroe's face tensed as he seemed to listen on his headset. "No. Negative. Will not alter my flight plan, Long Bow. Repeat. Negative."

A flash of fire ripped in front of the S-92.

"What the hell are you doing, Long Bow! I am a private helicopter on a private flight. You are breaking all flight protocol."

Monroe looked at Annie. "He's a madman." He seemed to be listening again. "Negative, Long Bow. Will not reroute to Canyon Lake. You must wave off and allow me to proceed unhindered—or face FAA sanctions and criminal penalties."

When Annie heard that, she thought it must be Eli in the Long Bow.

Another flash of fire in front of them. Monroe said, "This guy's an absolute madman," and he veered the S92 toward the east mountains.

"Seems you've met your match, Monroe." Annie laughed. "I'd listen to him if I were you."

"Shut up." He flipped a switch on the instrument panel and said, "Calling Maricopa County air support. This is Houston Monroe. I'm being fired upon by an AH-64D Apache Long Bow attack helicopter. Request urgent assistance. Repeat: This is Houston Monroe and I'm being fired upon by an AH-64D Apache Long Bow attack helicopter. Request urgent assistance."

Another flash of fire shot over the S-92's windshield. Monroe mumbled, "A madman. All right. All right. He wants to go to Canyon Lake. I'll go to Canyon Lake. Let's see if he can follow me through the canyons. Ha." The S-92 circled back and shot through the narrow sheer-faced canyons twisting and turning at breakneck speed, Annie gripping the sides of her seat. "That should do it," Monroe said and he laughed. "I knew he couldn't stay with me through here."

The Long Bow pulled up alongside Annie's window. Eli sat comfortably in the helicopter. He smiled and gave Annie a thumb's up.

"He's a madman!" Monroe said when he saw Eli. "But I'll tell you one thing—he can't match speed. This is one of the fastest helicopters in the world. It'll blow his Long Bow away." Monroe veered out of the canyon and headed for open air space. "Ha ha. See you later, madman."

Annie unbuckled her seat belt. "Don't let me slow you down." She grabbed at the control stick Monroe had his hand on.

The helicopter spun wildly to the right. "What the hell are you doing!"

Annie slapped him. His sunglasses went flying. "Slowing you down."

"You'll burn for this! You'll spend the rest of your life in prison!"

She slapped him and grabbed the stick again, the chopper nearly going into a spin. When the helicopter stabilized, two more missiles flashed in front of it. "You can do what you want to me, Monroe, but if *you* want to live, I think you'd better obey the madman."

Monroe seemed to be listening long and hard on his headset. He narrowed his eyes at Annie. "He doesn't know who he's dealing with. He's going to pay. You're both going to."

Annie mock shuddered and climbed back into her seat.

Monroe sighed and said into his mic: "Roger, Long Bow, will honor your request to land in field adjacent to the steamboat ride at Canyon Lake. Request in turn you cease firing."

As the S-92 banked back toward the steamboat ride, Annie saw four helicopters flying into the canyon. Three had TV news logos on their sides. One a sheriff's star.

Monroe hovered the S-92, beginning his descent onto the

field next to the steamboat ride, a tremendous dust cloud rising. Annie saw the Long Bow veer off and disappear over Superstition Mountain.

“Well, it seems,” Monroe said, the helicopter lowering, one landing skid contacting the ground, then the other, its blades powering down but still spinning, “since Sheriff Delgado may be a little late to the party that I’m going to have to search you myself.” He unbuckled his seat belt and stood.

Annie gritted her teeth.

Monroe tried to slip his hand under her top. She punched him in the nose. He pushed her head back into the seat. She bit his hand. He jumped onto her and she shoved him to the floor. She stood. “You killed babies, Monroe. You were going to kill Chase. You’re a heartless coward is what you are.” She kicked him in the groin.

The other helicopters were landing, reporters with microphones, cameramen hustling, charging at the S-92, and a black Hummer turned hard onto the field. Annie reached under her shirt. She looked and Monroe straightened up. She kicked him in the groin again—harder. She reached under her shirt again and unclipped the memory card. She could see Thad, in dark sunglasses and a baseball cap pulled tight—Sheriff Delgado not far behind him—pushing through the reporters, inadvertently knocking over a cameraman, to get to the door Annie was opening.

Annie jumped down from the helicopter and was steadied by Thad as she landed. For the briefest of moments they held hands, Annie feeling the memory card leave her hand for his, and then Thad calmly turned and drifted back through the reporters and deputies.

# Chapter Twenty-four

Annie woke in a dark cell, or she'd been woken. She couldn't be sure. Her mind wasn't quite her own yet. She knew she'd been arrested at Canyon Lake after the helicopter flight and put in Sheriff Delgado's lockup. Deputies had searched her, pushed her around, told her she'd spend the next thirty years in prison, and then when she'd finally been left alone, she'd drifted in and out of chaotic nightmare-strewn sleep. Only one thing was certain—life as she knew it was over. The thought of spending thirty years in prison was something she couldn't handle thinking about, but when she'd wake and realize where she was she couldn't help but think about it. Then the stress of thinking about it would short circuit her mind and she'd fall back asleep. Only to be tormented by the nightmares.

Finally, mercifully, morning came, a gray light overcoming the cell: her bunk, a stainless steel toilet and little else. When her mind finally cleared enough to think lucidly she thought of Chase. She hoped her message from Stony Peak had been heard. She hoped the memory card she'd given Thad had captured Monroe's incriminating remarks. She hoped Chase was safe.

She sat up on her bunk. For the first time she realized she was wearing gray and white horizontally striped tops and bottoms—prisoner garb. Yes, it was no dream, she told herself. Strange as it might seem, it had all happened. And now she was going to have to pay the price. She swallowed hard and clung desperately to her hope that Chase was safe. It was all that was keeping her going.

A deputy, brown shirt, badge, dark slacks and a crew-cut,

walked up to her cell. "Get up." He put a key in the lock and turned it.

Annie didn't move. She'd read news reports of Sheriff Delgado's prisoners being beaten, being forced to do hard labor in a hundred and twenty degree heat, of being sexually abused by guards. "Why?"

The deputy glared at her, the lines on his face hardening as he approached. "Because I said so."

Annie knew enough from talking with Tara's lawyer-father not to admit to anything before speaking with an attorney. "I want to talk to a lawyer."

"People in hell want ice water. Now get up."

She had no choice. She rose and when she did, the deputy grabbed her elbow. It felt funny walking in the too-big prison-issue shoes. "Where are you taking me?"

The deputy said nothing as they walked down a corridor to a little room with the top half of its door open. Another deputy came to the door. The deputy with Annie said, "Prisoner Ann Rebarchek."

The new deputy, young-ish with acne, held out a form and a pen to her. "Sign at the x's," he said and he motioned with the pen, "here, here and here."

Annie shrugged. "What am I signing?"

The young-ish deputy looked at the other deputy, then said blandly, "Release papers."

Annie's eyes widened as she stared at the form. It did indeed look like a release form. Was this some sort of joke? Or maybe it was the release for getting out on bail? She signed and after she did, the young-ish deputy disappeared into the room and returned with a clear plastic bag with Annie's clothes: the plaid top, the calypso pants, the high-tops.

The escorting deputy said, “I’m assuming you’ll want to change.”

“Yes.”

The deputy led her to a small closet-size room where she changed—quickly.

The deputy then led her down yet another corridor and stopped at an open door of an office. A uniformed man sat behind a desk. “Sergeant Geary,” the escorting deputy announced to the man, “this is prisoner Ann Rebarchek presented for pre-release identity verification.”

The sergeant rose and walked to Annie. He put his hands on his hips and scowled at her. The look on his face was so hate-filled Annie thought he might hit her, but he just said, “Identity confirmed.”

The deputy tugged Annie down the corridor to a door with a wire-reinforced window. A black female deputy waited on the other side.

The deputy with Annie unlocked the door and giving Annie a little shove said, “Prisoner Ann Rebarchek presented for release.”

Annie hurried through the door, glancing back over her shoulder. She then walked with the black deputy, who said nothing, down yet another corridor to a beige metal door. The deputy pulled an expanding key chain from her service belt, put a key in the lock and turned it. She opened the door and said, “You’re free to go.”

The door opened to a simple room, folding chairs along yellow walls, a long card table, a ceiling fan just barely turning, but all Annie really saw were the people: her father and Tara, and standing a little farther off, Thad and Eli.

Tara ran to her and hugged her. “Oh my God, Annie! I’m so glad you’re okay!”

Annie could feel the tears coming. “Tara,” she said, but that was all she could get out, her freely flowing tears choking her voice.

“That’s okay,” Tara said, “you deserve a good cry.”

Annie’s father joined the hug, saying, “I love you, honey.”

Annie threw one arm around her father but her crying only intensified. Her chest was shaking.

“It’s all right, sweetie,” her father said. “You’re safe now. You’re safe.”

“But…” Annie tried to speak but the tears won again. She took some deep breaths. “…but…Chase? Is he okay?”

“Chase is fine, honey. He’s safe and sound,” her father said, then he turned and nodded toward Thad and Eli. “Annie, two of your friends are here. And from what I’ve heard, they’re very special friends.”

Annie wiped her eyes. She walked to Eli and hugged him. “Thank you so much, Eli.”

Eli smiled. “See, things have a way of working out, don’t they?”

She nodded and turned to Thad. “Thank you, Thad. Thanks for everything.” She so wanted to kiss him but because her father, Eli and Tara were there, she just gave him a hug—but she kissed him with the look in her eyes. “So,” she said, her eyes locked on his, “the memory card?”

“Uh.” Thad hesitated.

Annie’s warming heart cooled in a flash. If the information about Monroe’s abusing Chase didn’t get out there, Chase was still going to be vulnerable, maybe killed. Her eyes searched

Thad's.

"Uh," he repeated. He looked around. "This probably isn't the best place to discuss it."

She swallowed but then nodded and turned back to her father and Tara. "Come on. Let's get out of here."

A warm morning sun bathed the valley as they walked down the street to a park, where palm trees, bending and green, stood out against the brilliant blue sky. They found a concrete bench in a shaded area to sit. Annie's father put his arm around her, while Tara sat on the other side and held her hand. Eli and Thad were bookends.

Annie's breathing quickened. Her heart raced. Despite what her father had said about Chase, she felt as if she was being prepared for some terrible news about him. "What's going on? Somebody please tell me."

"Annie," her father said. "I've been keeping our attorney informed of everything. He says you're not to say anything to anyone. If someone insists on talking to you, just tell them to talk to him."

"And my father said," Tara chipped in, "he'll help any way he can."

"Hey, that's great." Annie squeezed her friend's hand. "But I want to know about Chase. Please tell me about Chase." She leaned forward and looked at Thad. "Did the memory card work out? Did the information about Monroe's abuse get out there?"

"My Peace Corp contact got it and forwarded it to all the U.S. Senators. Then the wire services picked it up." He smiled. "Annie, it went viral."

"And so Chase is safe now? Where is he? Who has him?"

"He's with the Department of Child Safety," Thad said. "And

they will place him with a loving family."

"Oh." She frowned. She didn't want Chase in one of those places.

"DCS is a good, caring organization, honey," her father said. "It's the best place for Chase right now."

"It's excellent," Thad added. "I checked it out. Thoroughly."

Annie exhaled deeply. "And they won't let Monroe have him?"

Thad shook his head. "Not after hearing the incriminating statements he made on the memory card. Absolutely no chance."

Annie caught his eye. "I want you to follow up on Chase, Thad, to keep track of him, to make sure he's safe and happy, always."

"*We* will, Annie. *We* will."

*We* always sounded so good, especially coming from Thad, but she knew he'd misspoken because she wasn't going to be able to do anything from prison, which is where she was headed for a long, long time. But she was breathing easier knowing Chase was safe. She remembered how tightly he'd held her, his precious little blue eyes calling out to her for help.

"So," her father said, "aren't you wondering how you got out so soon?"

"Oh." Annie swallowed hard, remembering all the things she'd done, all the trouble she must be in. She supposed her father with the help of his attorney must've posted bail fast. "I'm not sure I want to know any details yet, Dad. It's all still kind of overwhelming to me. The sheriff's deputies were telling me I was going to get thirty years and it was just about sinking me."

"Thirty years?" Her father looked surprised.

Annie sighed. Could it be more? Monroe had said she'd get

life. Oh, she was going to have to face the music soon enough, oh God—she took a deep breath—it might as well be now. "Is my trial date set yet?"

Her father looked at her. "There's no trial, Annie."

"Well, first court date, preliminary hearing, grand jury? I don't know the legal terms."

"There's none of that, honey."

Annie squinted at her father. "Aren't I out on bail?"

He shook his head. "No, honey. You're just out period. You're free."

Annie slumped and tears welled in her eyes. "Daddy, don't tease me."

"I'm not, sweetheart. You're free. Absolutely free."

"It's the truth, Annie," Thad said with a nod.

"Oh my God." Annie cried long and hard. Finally she found the strength to speak. "But how?"

Her father rubbed her arm. "The county prosecutor evaluated the evidence and decided he didn't have enough to prosecute you."

"Unreal." Annie wiped her eyes.

Eli spoke up. "It didn't hurt that millions of people were clamoring for your release."

Annie shrugged. "What do you mean?"

Thad leaned over and caught her eye. "Like I said the memory card went viral. When people realized what had really been happening, they turned on Monroe. And you…" He smiled. "…you've become a hero to them."

Annie smirked. "Yeah right."

Thad nodded. "You have."

"Dad." Annie hugged her father. "And, Tara, do you think I

could have a few minutes alone with Eli and Thad?"

"Sure, honey." Her father stood. "Come on, Tara."

"I won't be long. I love you," Annie said as they walked off.

Annie turned to Eli. "Thank you so much, Eli. You saved my life up there in the skies over Canyon Lake."

Eli shook his head. "The Great Spirit saved you."

"Well…"

"It was your wanting to do good that the Great Spirit honored. Just remember, Annie, when you want to do good, and you never give up even when things go against you, the Great Spirit will always find a way to help. You can count on it."

Annie slid over and gave him a big hug and a kiss on the cheek. "I thank the Great Spirit for you, Eli."

Eli teared up. "Well," he said, his voice cracking. "I guess it's time this old helicopter pilot got back to see if anybody needs help getting off the mountain." He wiped his eyes, rose and walked off.

Annie went to Thad. She took both his hands in hers and sat next to him. "Can I kiss you?"

He leaned into her and kissed her. Then he slipped her hands, lifted her onto his lap and took her in his arms. He kissed her again and pulled her tight against him.

"Tell me this is all really happening, Thad. That it's not a dream."

He smiled. "It's no dream, Annie."

"And Chase is really going to be okay?"

He nodded.

"And what's going to happen to Monroe?"

"He's in jail. Where he should be. He faces a host of charges. Charges even his money can't buy him out of. Vivian Sanchez and others that have been intimidated by him in the past are coming out of the woodwork to testify against him."

"And what about you, Thad? What are your plans?" She held her breath as she waited.

"You're my plans, Annie." He kissed her. "Maybe I'll be your manager. What I was saying earlier about you being a hero—you could go on all the talk shows, become a reality TV star."

She laughed. "All I want is my old life back." She gazed into his eyes. "And you."

He smiled. "I don't know after all you've been through if you'll be able to get your old life back. I don't know if you'd want it back. Me, though, you can have."

"And do you want me?"

He kissed her cheek, her lips, put his cheek next to hers, held it there and whispered in her ear, "I love you, Annie."

Annie closed her eyes and smiled.

The End

# About the Author

Gregg Bell writes suspense. Suspense loaded with intrigue and excitement but lacking gratuitous violence, sex and profanity. Gregg likes reading books that entertain but also challenge him and would like to think he writes the same. He was born in Chicago, Illinois. He's done everything from selling puka shells on the beach in Florida to working for Sears in their corporate headquarters at Sears (now Willis) Tower. A lifelong Midwesterner he lives in suburban Chicago. He's a biking enthusiast, a photographer, and insists he would be a good golfer if only he could putt.

Web Site:
greggbell.net

# Also by Gregg Bell

## *The Find*

What can a mother do when she has no money and a dangerously sick kid?

She can make a mistake.

In a moment of desperation, cleaning lady Phoebe Jackson tries to pawn the diamond-bejeweled Rolex she found in a mobster's locker. Turns out the watch is a fake, but the mobster isn't—and he's on to her.

## *American Ballerina*

Lily Russell thinks she can dance at London's prestigious Royal Ballet. She also thinks she can single-handedly bring about world peace. Her friends know she's delusional; her former bosses think she's unreliable. The only person who seems to believe in her is her jealous ex-lover, Jeremy, and he's shiftless and violent and doesn't seem to understand the concept of "ex." That doesn't stop Lily from dreaming; dreams make life an adventure. But when she meets Edmund, a man who seems to genuinely care for her and steadies her thinking, she starts to realize that her ordinary life might be enough of an adventure for her.

Lily expects a scene when Jeremy finds out about her new boyfriend, but she never could've expected the brutal murder that shakes her to the core. Now the police want her for questioning. The men in her life say they want to help her but can she trust them? Soon it becomes apparent the police think she's the killer, and, her feeble grip on reality fading fast, Lily's not entirely sure she isn't.

## *Jamie's Gamble*

Jamie Thompson's never been good at taking chances. Young, beautiful and from a wealthy family she's had little reason to. She has it all. Everything but what she values most—her freedom. So she counts the cost and flees to a Texas border town where a friend has set up a job for her.

What she didn't count on is meeting Ricky Benson. Ricky's dream of pitching in the big leagues shattered by an injury, he's killing his disappointment with booze and blondes. Jamie knows he's trouble, but she sees the good in him too. The shocking crime that happens next tests her new-found freedom and threatens her growing love for Ricky.

Life is a gamble, Jamie's finding out fast, and she discovers that for love she may have to risk it all.

## *The Test*

It's the last chance for law intern Mary Maloney. Twice she's failed the bar exam and if she fails again, she'll lose her job, her home, and her self-respect. Only love keeps her going, but that too seems to be slipping through her fingers.

Tom Falcone has always "the guy" for Mary. He's kind,

thoughtful, wants a family, and he's all Mary ever wanted. But has she managed to alienate him just when she needs him most?

Now, needing everything she's got to come through, a stunning revelation sends her reeling. The life she's always dreamed of is still within reach, but only if she can somehow pass one final test.

## *Man of God*

Once he was a gentle soul, a man of peace, but after thirty years of ministering in his gang-infested Chicago neighborhood, Reverend John Archer fantasizes about killing gang members. That's when he looks out the church window and sees a young boy shot in the head. He rushes to the police station and gives a sworn statement. Only when it's too late does he find out that the gang leader he identified is known for killing witnesses—and their families.

Archer scrambles to protect his wife and children, but before he can, a gang member abducts him. Archer prays desperately and believes he hears from God, but the answer surprises—the gang member, Billy, is sick of the gang leader's brutality too. Even more surprising, Billy’s heart seems to be softening, while Archer’s is hardening. The odd pair form an uneasy alliance and together come up with a desperate plan—but it's an ungodly one.

Saving Baby
Copyright © 2016 by Gregg Bell
Published by:
Thriveco, Inc.
207 North Walnut Street, Itasca, IL 60143


ISBN-13: 978-1543088700



06217

Cover design by Christine Savoie

Made in the USA
Columbia, SC
26 March 2023